Roundabout

Roundabout

Elaine Durbach

www.elainedurbach.com

Author: Elaine Durbach
Cover Design: Abigail Rothman
Motorcycle Drawing: Rick Parker
Book Layout Design: Linda Lombri, *Lombri Writes!*

This book is a work of fiction. The characters, incidents, and dialogue are drawn from the author's imagination unless otherwise specified in the text. Any other resemblance to events or persons living or dead is coincidental.

ROUNDABOUT

ISBN-13: 9798985883107 (paperback)
ISBN-13: 9798985883114 (ebook)

'Tis the gift to be simple
'Tis the gift to be free
'Tis the gift to come down where we ought to be,
And when we find ourselves in the place just right,
'Twill be in the valley of love and delight.

"Simple Gifts" – Shaker Hymn by Joseph Brackett

There is a time for everything...
A time to weep and a time to laugh...
A time to mourn and a time to dance

Ecclesiastes 3

Acknowledgments

Thank you!

First, to my husband, Marshall Norstein, who refused to read my work-in-progress, probably thereby saving our marriage, while keeping me nourished and sheltered. And to my son, Gabe, who gives me joy.

To Alison Blank, for the Latin quote that set me on the blissful path of fiction writing: *"Nulla dies sine linea"* – "No day without a line."

To the nurturing members of the Montclair Library WriteGroup novel critique group, without whom this might never have moved from mind to keyboard.

To my earliest readers and encouragers, among them (to name just a few) Sue Geller, Cyndi Freeman, Jennifer Resnick, Holly Scalera, Julie Burstein, Birgit Matzerath, and Lisa Trusiani, and my copy editors, Joel Fulon, Ruth Elwell, Alison Thomas, Zilla Goodman, and Abby Kanter.

To Elaine Bloom who pushed me past that point and into publishing.

To Linda Lombri, who turned the manuscript into a real book, and a big thank you to Rick Parker for the drawing of the motorcycle and to artist Abigail Rothman who wove it into her design for the cover.

And finally, to those who provided inspiration from our youth and friendship in the present, so that memories turned into this utterly different, totally fictional story. (Yes, all you who've asked – fictional!)

Dedication

For Jan, my sister - whose faith in my heart and mind
gave me the faith to write this story

~ 1 ~

His Pillow

My beloved departed in the pre-dawn hours this morning. I called. They came. They took him. Dust to dust, or ashes more likely.

Eventually, I climb back into bed, tightly swaddling myself in the quilt that's grown cold without body warmth. What else can I do? Not making calls yet. Too early to drop this pain into others' lives. My lungs feel stiff. The gale off the Atlantic Ocean is rattling the diamond-pane windows, pushing drafts through the warped frames. I should fix them. Felix won't — Felix wouldn't. Oh my God.

How the hell could you do this — exit, just opt out? You promised me...

Trying so hard to stay calm, to breathe, to clutch onto gratitude for the long years we've known each other, and for these blissful few we've finally had together. I was without him for so long, why should solitude be such a monstrous prospect?

We were together long, long ago, Felix and I, in this country at the tip of Africa. Then apart for way too long, and reunited at last, here on its southern edge. Still astounds me how two people who began with so much lust found each other again when that heat had faded to a glow.

I duck my head, imagine the warmth in the crook of his neck, the embrace of that still-strong arm around my shoulders, our bodies notching together as if made for each other. Even through the whiff of muscle ointment, the smell of him is pleasing. I wait for the rumble of voice in his chest, the usual "Good morning, Copper Girl. Ready for some coffee?" Listen for it. Listen.

The dip in his pillow is still there. Staring at it from my side, I see his leathery cheeks and teasing eyes looking back at me, the rumpled gray hair — and then the younger version, as I first saw him. Oh, was there lust!

We met on the first day of my last year of college. There he was in the long line that snaked all the way around the Administration Building, waiting — in our case — to register for physiology 101. It was just a whimsical choice on my part, an extra credit in a field I knew nothing about. For him it was huge, the next step in his laser-focused plan for a new career.

Standing in a shrinking patch of morning shade, I eyed the back of the head in front of me. The tawny strands looped over his khaki collar where most of the other boys still had neatly barbered napes and hair slicked with Brylcreem. I couldn't make out if the hair was blond or brown. He spun around as if he'd felt my gaze and peered down at me, his eyes flicking from my head and straight shoulders to my sandals and back up, before he began asking, "Where/What/How does this process work?"

I was used to people staring. My hair, snow white now, was auburn then, and I was very trim. But I wasn't used to being sized up so openly. He wasn't flirting, just taking me in. I stared back up at him but had a hard time focusing. He was like a tiger, light on his feet, totally aware. That kindled an awareness in me. I responded with fake poise, way less friendly than I'd been to everyone else around us.

What an unlikely pairing we were — me a virgin who'd never left home before coming to Grahamstown, that easily managed little college community, a sheltered Goody Two Shoes whose heart fluttered when a favorite professor rewarded me with a kind comment or an invitation to partake of sherry; Felix, a guy who preferred tequila, and at twenty-four had been with more women than he could remember.

He'd arrived on campus, I soon learned, after years of adventure, riding in on a motorcycle with stuffed panniers and a battered leather backpack. In it were his journals, a collection of mismatched, dog-eared notebooks that detailed his travels — and very little else. That gave me the notion that he didn't care about possessions — a total illusion.

∽

His journals are below me as I lie here in one of the boxes, stashed in the darkness under our bed. For so long I've itched to read them. I have so many questions, but I've respected his privacy too much to ask. As forthright as he was, Felix kept certain secrets hidden behind a prickly hedge of defensiveness.

Now, I suppose, I can read those journals. No reason not to, is there? It's a way to hear his voice instead of the silence.

Kneeling with my forehead pressed against the mattress, I maneuver the box closer. The spines are arranged in order, each inscribed in his wildly irregular script: number, year, place. I pull out one, "#3, 1965, India," and decipher the first line:

> *"Woke this morning and for a crazy moment couldn't remember the name of the lovely blond girl lying next to me."*

Oh, I hear his voice all right, and just like that the old dread flares. It feeds off my grief. For the past five years it's lain dormant, vanquished — I thought — by the joy of finally being together. By maturity. By security — the certainty that I was the woman he wanted to be with. But on this awful morning all it takes is that glimpse of a faded journal entry and this almost-seventy-year-old is turned back into a silly, vulnerable girl.

Was it my fault we didn't stay together in our twenties? Or that we didn't grasp our chance ten years ago on the New York shore when at last we were both free? Or was that because of demons of his own?

I want to scream. All these damn questions whining with the wind and no way to ask them now. No way to get answers.

But there are the journals.

↢

What hit me that first morning in Grahamstown was utterly unfamiliar. Our eyes met and a tingle zigzagged from my core to my extremities. I felt my cheeks flush.

"When this is done, let's go get some coffee," he said.

"Why?"

"You're right," His eyes — topaz then, honey brown as he grew older — glittered. Was he laughing at me? "Why would you with a total stranger? As a favor to me. I have so many questions, and you obviously know your way around this place. My treat?"

"Well, okay."

How could I refuse? It would have been rude. But as we walked out of the building half an hour later into the blaring heat, our forms and folders and curricula in hand, out of the corner of my eye I saw Felicity and her buddy, co-residents of the dorm where I was senior student. They tilted their heads together and giggled. *Bunnington is making a play for that bad-boy new guy. Ha! Good luck to him. Maybe he can defrost our ice maiden.* I didn't hear them, but I knew the gist of what they'd be saying.

&

Bunnington isn't my name. I'm Sally Paddington. They called me Bunnington back then because of the way I wore my hair, so neat, so proper. So unlike this unmoored crone adrift in this huge, empty bed.

I was in love with ballet, and though I planned a much more practical career as a music teacher, I still took dance classes off campus and, when the police didn't prevent it, taught a wonderful group of Xhosa children in the black

5

township on the far side of the valley. The old grooming habit prevailed, of scraping my hair back into the smoothest knot I could manage, to keep myself mindful of discipline and posture.

The nickname was fine. It was better than "Paddington Bear," which came later, after that dancer posture had given way to postpartum slouch, and long after Felix, my tiger man, had done his disappearing act.

In this wind-chilled room, almost five decades later, I taste again the bitterness of abandonment. *"Au revoir, not goodbye,"* he wrote, on a page torn from a calendar.

I didn't believe him, or I needed to not believe him. I kept my feelings as tightly under control as my hair. It was easier to keep drawing breath, to get up and go to work the next morning, if I accepted it was over forever, that I would never see him again.

I screwed up that page, November 1970, and hurled it at the waste basket. Missed. Kicked it away, out of sight.

But I was wrong; Felix was right. We would see each other again and again — and we would part again and again.

This time, not even an *"au revoir."*

Disbelief swells like the waves I can hear in the distance. It rises, curls over, and crashes, sweeping over me. I exhale hard, as if that will expel the pain — and for a long moment choose not to inhale. Intrigued by the notion of not continuing. Why should I? Who would be harmed if I don't?

That first coffee. He tilted a thumb towards the battered old motorcycle, parked just across the street from the Admin

Building, just letting me know it was his.

"We're going on that?" I wasn't sure if I wanted to or not.

"No way!" he said and started walking.

Subject closed. Immediately I wanted a reason, but he was a stranger. I remembered my manners. I scampered after him.

Time smooths some people, sands away their sharp edges and gives them gloss. It has roughened me up. I'm no longer that careful girl, proper as I may sound. Right now I want to run outside and down the cobbled street, screaming obscenities and rending my flannel pajamas. Felix — young and old — is laughing from the fake-wood rafters overhead, daring me to do just that. *You bastard!*

That January morning at Rhodes I led him down a gravel path edged with bright purple and white petunias, the college colors, to a neon-lit greasy-spoon cafe on the edge of campus. My toes pointed out — five-to-one, the dancer way. His, I noticed, turned in slightly; he walked with a rolling gait as if he'd just dismounted from a horse — or a motorbike? We slid into one of the booths, but as we did, the metal edge of the table raked my forearm. A row of tiny red dots emerged. He grabbed a paper napkin and gently dabbed the blood, the tendons on his tanned hand flexing over my pale, freckled skin. I don't remember any pain. My mouth made an "O" like a fish, and the openness traveled all the way down to a lower region I usually ignored. Beneath the table I clenched my thighs and hoped he didn't notice me blush.

Quite briskly with no more fuss, he looked around for a waitress.

"By the way, I'm Felix," he said.

"Bunn – er – Sally."

They say that there's no love like first love. That can be a negative as much as a positive, the same as it is with sex. It can be unforgettably exciting – more terrifying and transformative than any encounter after that. Or it can be a mess. And sometimes you don't know which it has been until a long, long time later. That day everything felt messy even after the bleeding stopped.

My cup tap-tapped against the Formica surface. My hands weren't shaking; they were vibrating. My whole body was. If I looked at this stranger, would he be vibrating too, staring at me? I finally risked it and found him staring down into the dark liquid as if trying to read his future. When he did glance up, shoving his streaky locks behind his ears, even in the neon glare he was shimmering.

I remember the coffee was awful. Despite how much we oldies love to moan about how everything is so much worse these days, some things have improved and coffee is surely one of them.

That thought gets me out of bed and into the kitchen, enveloped in Felix's scratchy wool robe. No hot cuppa yet and it's eight o'clock already. Habit prevails. As I switch on the coffee machine, our tabby, Mergatroid, pushes in through the flap in the back door, jubilant to find me ready to serve him. He winds around my ankles, and I spoon tuna from a can into his bowl. Has he noticed the absence? We haven't had him long, but there'll be one less body to snuggle up to, two hands fewer to pet him – the ones that would tickle his belly until he wrestled back, kicking with his back legs and play-biting, purring all the while.

He'd hover underfoot as we cooked breakfast together, hoping for tidbits. Felix made the toast while I fried mushrooms and stirred the scrambled eggs. I'd reach for two plates; Felix would unhook the mugs, choosing two from our ever-growing row of weird and wonderful creations.

Living alone, I used to read a newspaper while I ate. In this house, we turned on the radio and listened together to the morning news, exclaiming, arguing sometimes. The election news from the U.S. made him laugh and had me seething. "It's not funny!" I yelled a few times. "That guy could win!" On South Africa, we take opposite positions, me upbeat, reveling in the change from the evil ways of the old government – and Felix fuming. He has no time for the corruption of the new one – *had* no time. Oh, God, *had* no time.

"Those sons of bitches," I hear him say. "They're robbing us blind, stealing our future."

I wanted to make an excuse for their greed after all the years of oppression. He'd tell me I was too soft-hearted and tip my face up to give me an eggy kiss. I would butter him more toast and reach for more too, hungry as a teenager.

I want to tell Mergatroid the terrible news, to practice saying the words out loud – and can't. Just stroke him instead, from arching neck to tail tip, over and over, soothed by his contentment. It's only when I go to press the brew button that it hits me: Quantity – one cup.

❧

There we were, sipping hot, dark dishwater in the cafe. The only good part was the abundance of the stuff. The waitress, a big-bosomed black woman with a starched white apron and matching cap, came over to offer a top-up. I held out my cup and she snapped at me to put it down. "You don't want to get burned, do you?" She glared at Felix too, and he whisked his hands away, holding them open with a big feline grin. She simpered back and poured slowly up to the rim. I wanted to slap her dimpled face, and I didn't even know his last name yet.

Then he hunched over his cup, brushed his hair back and twinkled at me as the waitress walked away. "So, Sally, tell me your life story, starting now."

My life story starts now? I was under the impression it started twenty-one years ago, but I began telling him anyway — my set spiel about how I was born on a ship in the Mediterranean as my parents made their way to Palestine from war-battered Poland, and how after a few years they gave up the struggle to make a life in what had become Israel and ventured instead to the land of gold and diamonds.

Usually, that summary drew a "Wow!" and "Hell, my life's not that interesting." Not so with this guy. He told me he'd spent two months on a kibbutz, evidently unperturbed that he was one of the few non-Jews there, before heading to Turkey and India.

"Those Israelis are arrogant sons-of-bitches," he said. "But they're totally in touch with the land, and, I don't know, God? Most of the ones I met were atheists, like me, but they knew the Old Testament better than my parents, with all their damned preaching."

I declared I was an atheist too. I'd never said that to my parents – or anyone else, come to think of it. Wasn't even sure it was true but wanted to be on his wavelength. We went on to bemoan the racism of our awful government and how insular South Africa was. While our peers in America were breaking hearts and skulls over Vietnam, we were wrapped in our own obsession with racial injustice. It was comforting in a way – to see the U.S. taking heat from the international community, so we weren't the only baddies in the world.

"*Schadenfreude*," I said, and immediately regretted it. Being a brainiac. I muttered, cheeks hot again, "Taking pleasure in other countries screwing up. My parents speak lots of languages. I get it from them."

"I know what it means," he said, "but I sure as hell didn't learn it from my folks. I read a lot, and *ich spreche Deutsch*. Spent time in Austria and Switzerland and Germany."

That drew a "Wow!" from me. Even in that shabby café with the linoleum worn down to the floor boards and fly-speckled photos of old movies, he was swathed in the glamour of those places. He must have seen the Alps and ridden on the Autobahn and seen where Freud grew up. I wanted to travel abroad too – though with a tour group, not the way he had, alone, with no safety net. His worldliness was intoxicating, but it made me wary of seeming naïve. I listened in virtual silence.

"My surname is Barnard," he told me, and joked about being related to Dr. Chris Barnard, the swashbuckling heart transplant pioneer we both worshipped. In his case, it was more than idolizing; he wanted to be a life saver too.

I also wanted to do good, but hadn't worked yet out what

11

what field it would be in. Could dance be a serious career?

At last he got me to talk too. I told him my last name, but skimmed over how, in South Africa, my parents chose it for themselves, replacing one that had four consonants in a row. We became the Paddingtons. What a bizarre choice for two Polish Jews, but no one told them that, and it served their need to paste over the nightmares of their past. It became their identity and mine of course, even as the food in our home stayed faithfully Polish.

"We Paddingtons live on borscht and boiled tongue," I remember telling Felix. "For all her best efforts, my mother makes the most awful roast beef." He laughed at that and murmured that any home cooking sounded good to him. For a moment I imagined cooking pierogis for him the way Imma had taught me. I'd never cooked for a boy before.

Ah, Imma and Pops. I wrap my arms tight around my ribs. Ache adds to ache. Till now, those two losses have loomed as my most agonizing brushes with death. But even in the depth of misery there was acceptance. Children expect to lose their parents. There was even gratitude, that they had outwitted a fate that might have taken them decades earlier in terror and violence. As Jews request of God, their memory has been a blessing.

Morning # 3 A.F. – After Felix. It dawns on me: Is our first encounter described in his journals? I don't know when he stopped writing them. Coffee mug in hand, curiosity sparked, I pad down the passage to the bedroom. Bright beams of sunshine are slicing across the purple and red Indian textile on the wall above our pillows, shooting sparks of light off the sequins. He acquired it on a business trip and was delighted when I found it among his possessions and suggested we hang it. We clicked like that every now and then, our tastes overlapping just when least expected. Neither of his ex-wives had liked it.

Sitting down on my side of the bed, still careful not to disturb his blankets, I push aside a novel on my bedside table to make room for the mug and reach down to the journals. From this angle, a second box blocks the one I want. I can feel the fine grain of dust covering tightly packed files. I don't know what they're about – probably his old academic material – and right now I don't care, except that it's heavy and in the way. What I want is more of young Felix, my gallivanting boy out in the world, and I tug hard to free up the journal container. Big mistake. The stretch sends a needle of pain through my hip joint.

The book closest at hand is the last one: "#5, 1967, Brazil." There's something else scratched in after Brazil but it's too smudged to make out. Nothing about 1968? So he stopped writing the diary when his travels ended, before me? My solar plexus aches. What am I hoping for – some sweet term of endearment, some postscript to prove our bond was special from the start?

Again, I rear back. Not ready to face an ending of any kind. Back goes #5 into its slot and out comes book "#1, 1963, France." I plump up my pillow and reach for his to get double support, and lean back, ready to start reading. Just another few minutes of procrastination before I make myself get going on the morning's chores.

As I lift my cup I realize what I've done. The dip in his pillow is gone. With the imprint of my body I have erased his. Cross-legged, I double over, inflamed hip be damned, finger tips pressing against eyelids, trying to keep the flood at bay.

~ 2 ~

Desks

Day # A.F.? I'm losing count. Nine or ten?

A real estate agent knocked on the door this morning. So darn rude! Uninvited and unwelcome. I wasn't even dressed yet. Answered the door in my flannel pajamas, thinking it would be one of the neighbors.

I stood there with shoulders hunched, trying to keep chilled nipples from showing through the daisy-dotted fabric. He yammered about "the terrific potential," real-estate-agent-speak for "in need of renovation." That's undeniable. It's a shabby old cottage with hokey nautical décor. He'd seen the plaster mermaid reclining above the front door, and was peering over my shoulder into the kitchen, probably noting the wall tiles with anchors on them, and the light fitting made from a ship's wheel. This is how it was when Felix bought the place, and bit by bit we'd been making it ours, repairing and updating, but we had a long way to go. The kitchen was next on our list.

It's too damn soon to discuss prices and marketing, I told the guy, and politely suggested he get lost. I can't make these decisions on my own anyway. He apologized for jumping the gun and asked me to hold onto his card for when I'm ready.

His visit has left me quivering. I have to face this but that calls for strength, and my bones feel hollow. The money from the sale is earmarked for his kids as per Felix's will, drawn up before I re-entered his life. We should have looked ahead, I suppose, made plans for future possibilities, but I didn't want to think ahead. It was miracle enough that we were finally together. And even if he had suggested changing his will, I would have insisted that the house go to his kids. After all, we weren't married. Making vows hadn't worked all that well for either of us, so why tempt fate?

But what now? Shoving some of his paperwork aside, I settle at his desk, find a working pen and yellow legal pad, and try to make a list of my assets.

Odd how I'd never gotten around to creating desk space for myself, though Felix asked where I would like to work. Not sure which room would be most conducive and haven't had the urge or the focus to get back to my writing. It calls for withdrawal, and being with him — sharing in the gardening or cooking or doing repairs — or simply sitting in side-by-side deck chairs soaking in the sunshine, hands linked — has filled me with satisfaction.

I have some funds of my own, thanks to book sales, bonds my parents left me, and rent from my little place in New York. Not sure how much it all amounts to but clearly it's not enough to buy this house, not if I also want to eat as I grow older.

My eyes close. Pathetic, but for a moment I see the curtain rise on the final scene of *Swan Lake*, and the, heartbroken swan princess leaping to her end. I danced that role when I was 18, and muscle memory still contains every step. She led the way, to be followed by her prince. Maybe I can have a burst aneurism too and be done with this. Some days I fancy such an exit. Quick and easy. *She lowers her smooth head with the coronet of feathers between her outstretched arms, pinky fingers slightly arched...*

Standing up from his desk, I catch sight of my reflection in the glass on the picture above it. Ghostly over the familiar *Guernica* print, there's this mad woman with a pale mop like mist around her head. Very un-swanlike. Can't remember when I last put on makeup or tamed my hair. There are snarled parts I vaguely pass over with a brush, or simply twist up and fasten with a big clip. When Felix was here, I dressed carefully, not like Miss Prissy from our student days but at least with a bra. *Tomorrow*, I keep thinking, *Tomorrow I'll do better*. I'll untangle my hair. Or chop it off. It'll fall like the snow we never see here, like the snow I remember from New York. I wish I'd stayed there and never agreed to come here to him.

All through our two years together in Grahamstown I wore my hair drawn back sleek and tidy when Felix wasn't around. When he was, it usually ended up a wild red tangle that took ages to unknot. He delighted in feeling for the pins that held the bun and extracting them one by one, watching as the coil sprang loose.

The first time he did that was just weeks after we met. His warm fingers caressed my neck, and a look of wonderment swept over on his face. The old images come poking through the reality of this wind-rattled cottage in Kalk Bay, in suburban Cape Town. Instead I'm back on the Rhodes campus, faded as old sepia photos, gradually filling in with color. If I can focus the lens of memory clearly enough, might there be answers to the querulous doubts that have begun jabbing at me, keeping me awake?

Did he really care? If he did, shouldn't he have considered my security? If I was special to him, why did it take so long – and such a crisis – to ask me to come stay with him?

Lying in bed last night, listening to the thud of distant breakers against the sea wall, I remembered another shore and big, uplifting waves. A weekend together with hopes so high for something more. Anger swells – at him and at myself.

There was no plan to get together after our initial coffee, just a "See you around" from him, and a "Good luck with everything" from me. But then we crossed paths coming out of a physiology lecture and started chatting as we crossed the quadrangle to our respective second classes.

"You looked perplexed," Felix said. "I was watching you as Prof Harding drew that diagram of muscle structure on the board." He was watching me, really? My heart did a little pitter-patter. He had haunted my thoughts since our first encounter, but I assumed he'd forgotten all about me. "Are you clear how the fibers work?" I wasn't at all. He was correct; I'd been confused. "Would you like me to go over it with you? This stuff has always fascinated me."

In the ten minutes between classes, we sat on the edge of the walkway, legs stretched out in the sun, his heavy textbook spread open on his left thigh and my right one. I tugged at my miniskirt but I could feel his jeans rub against my skin, and battled to concentrate.

A week later we met to work on an assignment at a pizza place on High Street. I insisted it was my treat, given that he was helping me and clearly didn't have much cash. Across the table, my eyes kept settling on his fingers, and his square wrists, and the muscles of his arms. His hand brushed mine as he walked me back to the dorm, and I wished he would grasp it, but he didn't.

He told me a little more about his travels and asked more about my background. I told him my parents weren't expecting to find gold in South Africa, but as teachers — he of Ancient History and she of French, and both reasonably fluent in heavily accented English — they expected enough people would pay for their services.

"And they did?" Felix asked. I nodded.

I'd grown up in one of the "whites-only" suburbs of Cape Town, a day's train ride from Grahamstown, in a home that was modest but stable. I had piano lessons and ballet, of course, and everything I ever needed, except a sibling or any other relatives. In my parents' world — and therefore in mine — those you love can disappear forever and had done so. I didn't mean to go into all that, but faced with his boldness, there was this strange urge to present my truth, to let him know the source of my caution. I'd broken the law a number of times, I told him, doing things like going to concerts in the "Colored" areas where we whites weren't meant to go, or deliberately sitting towards the back of the bus, alongside dark-skinned passengers. Sounded so lame compared to what he'd probably done, but defying apartheid was the one type of rebellion my parents condoned. We were the good people in a world that contained Nazis and the monsters of apartheid. That meant proudly thumbing our noses at segregation – but not at anything else.

In all other respects, the Paddingtons were respectable, respectful people, lest we attract any dangerous attention. Imma and Pops did their best to convince me risk-taking was overrated. I breathed in their anxiety. Until meeting Felix, I had stepped cautiously through my fragile world, mindful always that life can be cruel, that people you love can disappear without warning, be taken, vanish, leave you for no good reason at all.

The following Saturday, we went to a free movie the film society was showing, a Claude Lelouch. In the darkness, his bony fingers finally interlinked with mine, his thumb gently rubbing my index finger. I'd held hands a hundred times before, but this time it gave me a rush of pleasure. Half way through, we shifted in our seats and he put his arm around my shoulders. That was nice, but my hand felt cold. I wanted more skin contact. The movie was subtitled. He knew a bit of French and was amazed by my fluency. If he took it as boasting, he didn't seem turned off by it as other boys might have been. But then he wasn't a boy; he was a man.

He was a man who didn't live in a dorm, those bastions of gender-segregated chastity. He boarded with one of his professors, and suggested we meet there to study. I cringed at the thought of entering by the front door and risking an encounter with the old guy or his wife, but Felix assured me we could come in via a back entrance without being seen. In any case, he said, Mrs. Buchowsky was so absent-minded, she'd probably think I was his sister. He'd told her he had a few.

What was there to be embarrassed about anyway? We were just going to study together.

The first time we just necked.

It was a Friday afternoon, with shadows dappling the sidewalk as we walked from campus up to the Buchowskys' house. Grahamstown was a quaint town, at least on the white side, full of grand private schools and brown-stone churches, with thick-walled cottages lining quiet avenues of oaks. Approaching the door, the air was filled with scent from a jasmine vine and the hum of insects.

It took a moment for my eyes to adjust from the bright back garden to the dim room. I saw a mess, his bed roughly made and his books arrayed higgledy-piggledy along a bookcase of pine planks and bricks. He had textbooks but also a surprising number of other books – on philosophy and psychology and religion.

I remembered him mentioning the "best thing about the room – it comes with free access to the family's books. And they love hearing my travel stories!"

The other furniture was dark and solid, probably in keeping with the rest of the house. Felix pointed out the adjoining bathroom (his own, what a luxury!) in case I needed it, and then went to the kitchen to find us something cold to drink. I looked around in search of telltale personal touches. There weren't many.

Who was this guy? Aside from a small print of Picasso's "Guernica" taped to the wall, the décor surely wasn't his – a framed botanical watercolor, a Rembrandt, a calendar with puppies. No family photographs. There was a threadbare rug, a dresser, a wide bed, and an imposing wardrobe with a full-length mirror that reflected a straight-backed girl in a yellow dress. Two pairs of freshly ironed bellbottom jeans lay over the back of the desk chair, and a neat pile of folded shirts was stacked on the seat. Not his doing, probably the family's maid. Even in the dorm, in those days of racial privilege, there was housekeeping staff who made our beds and did our laundry. Where would it be best to sit?

Felix came back with two frosted glasses of Coca-Cola and set them carefully on the edge of the desk. He grabbed the clothes and shoved them into a drawer, and said, "Come, you sit at the desk. I'll be okay standing. Ignore the mess." He opened the textbook to the section we were studying and, leaning over me, began skimming through what we'd covered in class until I stopped him at a point I couldn't understand. No funny business, just work, and gradually my awareness shifted from the heat of his body behind my shoulder to the intricacies of cell chemistry.

Suddenly he dipped his head, and his nose brushed my ear

lobe. He sniffed and asked, "What are you wearing? Charlie?" I was. "I would have thought you were more of a Chanel girl." I shrugged and muttered something about wearing whatever I'd received for my birthday. I wanted him to sniff more.

He spun me around to face him, looked into my eyes, and, with his hand cupping the back of my head, slowly brushed his mouth across mine, lingered for a moment, and withdrew. He went back to reading aloud from the book, as if nothing had happened.

I sat for a minute with my lips tingling and couldn't take the longing anymore. I stood up, rising against him as he straightened, and kissed him hard on that curling mouth of his. His fingers slid down my rib cage to my waist, almost circling it, and settled on my hips. Then one hand went up to my hair. Down came the coil and he buried his face in the mass. I felt the rounded bulk of his shoulder muscles and the swoop of his spine. That open-down-below sensation was back, in need of pressure. My knees were shaking. I wanted to get under his shirt, to feel the groove between his pectoral muscles, but was mindful that if I did, he would reach under my blouse, or start undoing it, and that mustn't happen, shouldn't happen. My mother's anxious green eyes hovered in my mind like the Cheshire Cat's, minus the grin.

I turned away from him, trying to catch my breath, and took a sweet gulp of Coke. "We should get back to work," I said, twisting my hair up and searching unsuccessfully for the pins. It tumbled loose again.

He smoothed a strand back from my ear. "If you say so."

But first I wanted to know about the weird sketches lying

his desk, like plans for sci-fi body parts, and some of the books on his shelf — the odd collection with something handwritten up the spines, a number, a year, a place. He'd been so willing to discuss his travels, but he seemed reluctant to speak about his family. I gleaned the fact that he was one of four or five kids, that he'd grown up on a farm outside Durban.

That part sounded wonderful. I had wanted siblings so much, for a couple of years in grade school I kept a secret journal detailing daily adventures with a fictional older brother and younger sister. I even found photographs in a magazine that looked like how I imagined Jeffrey and Betsy and collaged them with a picture of me. The three of us tackled bullies, and formed a famous dance troupe, and persuaded my parents to let us go camping at a game reserve, even with the insects and wild animals.

Felix's family had seen real wild animals on their farm — monkeys and warthogs and hyenas. His family sounded so much more typically South African and normal than mine. His father didn't cry out in his sleep, I bet, and his mother surely didn't dress up as if every appearance was a celebration of survival.

But they weren't all that normal. "We kept moving, every time my dad came up with another of his big schemes," Felix said. "First he got tired of farming and started a business in Jo'burg. That went bankrupt and then he dragged us to Port Elizabeth. My poor old mom!"

Felix's father set up yet another venture there, this time selling religious tomes door-to-door. He'd been "saved," apparently. A tragedy of some kind had occurred, and the whole family joined a fundamentalist religious group. Felix refused, declaring himself a non-believer, and left home without finishing high school. "That was six years and almost four months ago," he said. "My father said I was damned and I better straighten out before I ever darken his door again."

He entwined his fingers in my hair and turned them this way and that so it caught the sunlight from the window. "It's so beautiful, like copper," he murmured.

I brought him back to the story. His voice was hoarse. "I thought my mom would try to make me stay. I would have. She'd already been through so much heavy stuff. I didn't want to give her more heartache." Very deliberately, he tried to make the textbook stand upright. It crashed over, knocking down my empty glass. "But she took my dad's side. She said I'd always been a handful, and I should go before I started giving the little ones dangerous ideas. So I buggered off." Those last four words dropped into silence. There was a raw pain that made me want to reach out with comfort, but there was a no-go zone around him. My first glimpse of the bramble hedge.

Abruptly, he brightened, poured half his drink into my glass and "toasted" me. I didn't dare ask anything else, but I assumed he and his parents eventually must have made up. Port Elizabeth is less than two hours from Grahamstown. Surely he'd go visit his family now. And maybe I'd meet them some time, like for Sunday lunch or a concert. Though I fought with my parents — my mother especially could drive me nuts — we never stayed cross. I wished she and Pops were nearby.

Felix told me he hitchhiked to Cape Town, this city where we finally landed up together. Strange to think we'd both been here as kids, he fending for himself at seventeen, me wrapped up in school and ballet. If our paths had crossed, would we even have liked each other? Probably not. He'd have scared me, with his raw independence.

"I lied about my age and got work as a bouncer, then as a bartender," he said, ticking off the jobs on his fingers, "then a handyman, and then selling shoes. Stayed wherever I could, in boarding houses, or on people's floors, and even now and then camped on the mountain with the *bergies*. They were kind, when they weren't blind drunk." He made it sound easy, but in those days in South Africa we privileged young whites were not supposed to be getting by that way. Most people – blacks and whites – would have been suspicious of him.

"And then I got lucky," he said, and his tone brightened. "I was hired as a driver-companion by this amazing, crazy inventor."

That man, John Latimer, changed his whole trajectory. He made him attend night classes and finish high school, and taught him how to measure and test and record experiments. "I learned scientific discipline from him, and I loved it," Felix said. "And he made me sign up to start doing a degree through Unisa, by correspondence." Mr. Latimer also bought him his first plane ticket. It was to Europe, with a mission to gather samples of products like those he was developing.

"I'd promised him that I'd keep up my studies and I did," he continued. "And I sent John the stuff he wanted, but I didn't come back. I just couldn't bear to cut short the wonder of it all." He peered at me, checking that I understood. "There was so much to see, so much to learn. So many people. I could be whoever I wanted."

⤬

Here, in his last home, I'm surrounded by the evidence of that passion. Felix might be gone but his books and his pictures and his precious mementoes are still telling his story. And they remind me of this one central fact: Felix was fascinated by the spectrum of humanity. Wherever he went he discovered characters who intrigued him and who, evidently, were just as intrigued by him, women most of all. It was as if he was always in search, and they wanted to be what he sought.

~ 3 ~

Dance Shoes

He didn't die on purpose, you know," my old pal Angie says.

My fault. She has a sharp tongue, always has had. I shouldn't have called her in such a whiny mood, but I've been drowning in the old doubts. This is Day #23 A.F., and my moods are fluctuating more than the erratic autumn weather, between devotion and icy, petulant resentment.

"If I knew he would up and leave, I'd never have come back to him," I'd said.

"Remember what drew you together in the beginning," she suggests, softening. "The bond was real. I saw you two, though I must say you were an odd combo back at Rhodes. I don't know who played harder to get, you or him."

She doesn't mean to make me sadder, but the reminder of those old games cuts through me. How many times did I try to get him to say, "I love you," without saying it myself?

"What does it mean anyway?" he would ask. "Can't you tell what I feel? Actions count more than words, and I show you, don't I? If it's not good enough for you..." Maybe he did show me, but my ego pined for reassurance, and those words are the gold standard. He would never utter them.

And now he never will, the son-of-a-bitch.

I was so sure that if I showed how much I cared, he would pull back. Was it anything he did or just the paranoia bred into my bones, a deep mistrust of fate? That's too rational a query for this staggering brain. Either way, now he has done the ultimate pull-back, and my only defense is to doubt everything.

"Take it easy on yourself, Sal," Angie says. "You know I don't advocate booze, but in your case, a stiff drink might be of help."

"Not before midday," I say, trying to lighten up. "Got to keep some discipline here."

We hang up and I go back to the chore I've set for myself today, tackling Felix's closet. I start with what I thought would be the easiest task, getting rid of his shoes.

It seems wrong to give them away, though there are homeless people down by the beach who might welcome them. The soles are molded by the shape of his feet, the hollows from the ball and the heel slightly deeper on the outer side because he was bowlegged, more so as he got older. That shaping could hurt someone with different balance.

Probably a lame excuse to hold onto them a little longer,

these ragged sneakers and worn-down moccasins and weathered boots, and one ancient pair of black lace-ups with a one-inch heel, still shiny under a film of dust. Where on earth do they come from and why did he have them?

The answer presents itself as if on command when I take a break at lunch time. In diary "#2, 1964, Spain," I learn for the first time that Felix studied flamenco dancing. Strange man; another of his secrets. Maybe he was loath to challenge me on my own turf, with dancing. Truth is, we did best when we pursued entirely different interests. Except for physiology, of course, where he was clearly in charge. The one time we tried to collaborate a few years ago, well, that didn't go so well.

He loved playing with different identities, and he was so light on his feet, it's easy to see how good he'd have been. I can just hear his heels thud against the floor strutting his stuff with some dark-haired *señorita*. He'd been picking olives, working on fishing boats in Moraira on the Costa Blanca, and then found himself a gig as a bartender through some friends in Barcelona.

> *"Have fallen in love with the gorgeous sexy dancing these people do and it turns out the manageress teaches it with a friend. Maria's giving me a special rate,"* he wrote. *"Every morning, I go for a lesson, Maria instructing and Lucia demonstrating with me. Afterwards we go eat lunch together. Then I fall asleep until it's time for work – siesta of course. How long can I stay? The government is uptight about foreigners. Afraid we'll incite a revolution?"*

He never did any flamenco with me, never mentioned

dancing with Maria.

On the next two pages, he had glued a note and a black and white photo. The note, I gather, was from his mother, wishing him a merry Christmas and saying she prayed for him every night, asking God to keep him safe. I assume John, the inventor in Cape Town, forwarded it. She made no request for him to come home, gave no news of his siblings, expressed no regret about the way she had banished him from the family. And yet, he'd kept that page, with its picture of hands clasped in prayer and a cross. Under it were two lines of writing scribbled over, as if he wrote and then thought better of it. About his mother? "*J...*" something, something I can just make out, "*would have loved the dancing here, like...figures...her music box.*" Or a girl who broke his heart, in Port Elizabeth or Cape Town, or on his travels?

The photo showed the festive interior of a bar, and a grinning Felix behind the counter, next to an older man and a lovely, smiling girl seated between them. Written underneath it: "*Great friends and colleagues, Jose and Maria.*" Satisfying to put faces to the names. And then I do a double take and look again: Is that *the* Maria? She's utterly unlike the sultry, brunette I've pictured all these years and of course speculated about. She has pale hair cut very neat and short, demure and sexy at the same time, like an exotic Julie Andrews.

Did she also teach him how to mix sangria? He certainly had the knack. Showed it off at a gathering we had out on the patio just a few months ago — in a different lifetime.

I sit back, daydreaming, which gives Mergatroid a chance to lie down across the page, purring expectantly. She is getting fatter by the day. Yes – she. No idea why we thought otherwise when she adopted us last year, pushing in through the old pet flap. Typical Felix, always attracting females. She is much more affectionate these days, sensing my need, or feeling her own.

The party day had been baking hot and even with the sun gone behind the mountain, the paving stones still radiated warmth. Felix whipped up a big, clinking bowl of cool yellow sangria spiced with his "secret ingredient," using oranges and limes donated by the neighbors, and juice from granadillas plucked from our own vine. It was ridiculously potent. Within an hour our friends were sprawled in drunken hilarity in the shaky old deck chairs, trying to outdo each other with tales of long-ago indiscretions.

"Well, you only live once," normally sensible Edith pronounced, remarking how sozzled she was. Her partner Roxanne was lying back in her chair, a hand resting heavy on each of their two chubby pugs. The only sober people were the three kids from next door, and possibly their mother, June. Zac, their dad, was doubled over, chortling at someone's joke.

I was a bit tipsy myself but very focused, traipsing barefoot from one to another, trying to refill glasses and offer snacks without spilling or dropping anything. Felix came up behind me, lifted my hair, and nuzzled my neck, wavering as he did so.

I smacked at him. "You realize this is your fault," I said, leaning back against his chest. "We're going to have to keep them all here to sleep this off."

"Everything is my fault, my beloved, and always has been," he declared. He snapped his snazzy suspenders, adopted since his waistline expanded, and then swayed off to put some more kebabs on the *braai*. Then he turned up the music.

For a moment I can smell the cindery steak and feel him behind me. What did he mean everything was his fault? Did I make him feel that way? Shove that thought aside, and cling for another while to the sounds and smells of that wonderful evening.

Finally, I yield up the shiny shoes. Dusted and de-cobwebbed, they go to my once-a-week gardener/handyman. Jacob, who is Xhosa, claps his hands and murmurs with delight. He has been glum all morning because we've had way too little rain and the plants surrounding the patio are turning brown. I should have been watering them, but I forget. Now he's beaming. "Oh, madam, these will be for my wedding. I will be very smart. Thank you, thank you." His gratitude is embarrassing.

Felix would probably have wangled an invitation to the wedding in the housing estate on the far side of the city, worn his boots, and danced the night away, arthritis and all. I would be scared to intrude, the white outsider. Felix had no such qualms.

My own dance shoes are stashed in my closet, untouched these past few weeks. My beloved pink satin toe shoes with their solid, blunt points are long gone. The current pair are just soft black leather. In my thirties, living in New York, I switched to modern and loved it almost as much, until I tore the meniscus in my knee. These days they'd probably have fixed me up as good as new. Not then – or not with the kind of health insurance I had. No great calamity. I can still walk for miles so long as I don't twist the wrong way.

But unless I'm demonstrating a step for students, I don't dance. Now and then, I'm lured in to conduct a session on world dance traditions with high schoolers, and once in a while – substituting for a friend – I teach little ones who're just starting out. You could eat them up, they're so cute, with their round tummies and wobbly legs. I clown around with some of the steps – a sight that would have scandalized my old teachers, and my old self – but they fall about laughing at my mistakes. And that frees them to take a chance themselves.

But because I can't move well, I'm inhibited in front of adults, even drunk ones. Pathetic, I know. Young Felix would have been on my case, mocking and challenging me to get over myself and have fun. But old Felix let me be, rubbed noses with me and went off in search of partners who were more game. And I watched him with pleasure. Not how young Bunnington would have reacted at all, or this neurotic self, piling old doubts on top of raw grief.

ᴥ

Young Bunnington was desperate to please Felix, but I had hurdles to overcome. Even with birth control pills and women's lib reaching us so much later than in Europe or the States, I agonized about giving my virginity to a guy who enjoyed women and didn't mention marriage. Initially, my reserve might have been a challenge – even heightened the attraction – and Felix would never have forced the issue, but eventually he would just have sidelined me to fond friendship and searched for someone more willing. I couldn't risk that. Girls fluttered around him in class and at the cafeteria, or when we hung out watching rugby matches. Even my closest pals,

34

Bev and Angie — though they denied it — looked up from under their eyelashes and cuddled up to him at the slightest excuse. Tiger blood had that effect, though sometimes it was more like tiger cub — so eager for that warmth. I decided not to give him cause to go looking.

It happened the fourth time we went to his room, on his twenty-fifth birthday. We also had our first fight that night. Like I said, love can be messy.

"What do you want for your birthday?" I'd asked the day before. We were snuggling together on a bench in the semi-privacy of a wisteria arbor behind the library. Felicity and a couple of her buddies swanned by, thankfully without seeing us. He needed all kinds of things — a new backpack, a better calculator (though he barely used the old one he had; math came easily to him), a bottle of tequila to replace the one he and his new buddies had drained, and definitely another pair of shoes.

"This is what I want," he said, sliding his hand up between my thighs. I was wearing slacks, but I jumped. I didn't push his hand away though; I held it, feeling the heat against my crotch, and just nodded. "Not if you're not ready," he said.

"I think I am. I'll see you tomorrow night."

Setting it up like that was so dumb. By the time I arrived at his door the next evening, with a bottle wrapped and be-ribboned, I was miserable with anticipation. He ushered me in, smiling and quiet, his hair damp and for once combed into some kind of order. I was thinking a drink might help, but he took the liquor and placed it on the book shelf behind him, and wrapped me in his arms.

"You could give a girl a chance to breathe," I stammered, but I was glad not to have time to think. He smelled wonderful, something cedary, maybe from aftershave, or just him. Things happened fast. Within minutes the pins came out of my bun, clicking on the floor. He gently pulled my hair to one side, and I felt the dress loosen as he drew the zipper down. He fumbled briefly with the three hooks of my bra and that loosened too.

"Please turn off the light."

He objected. "I want to be able to see you." But he reached out and flicked the switch off. The darkness was freeing. I let my dress and bra drop as he guided me to the bed. We lay down and I felt his hands traveling over my bare skin, stroking and caressing. He was muttering, "You're so beautiful, so damn beautiful."

"That's because you can't see me," I gasped, and shoved his shirt up, impatient to have it out of the way. He unbuttoned it and opened his fly and settled back against me.

"You are on birth control, aren't you?" he asked.

Oh, God — why would I be? Until the day before, I hadn't planned to do this. And now I really didn't want to stop. "Nah-uh," I muttered.

"Shit. Never mind. I've got a condom somewhere."

He sat up and began scratching around in his desk drawer. I took the opportunity to shed my panties. He shucked off his jeans and shirt, did something as he sat there, and lay beside me, guiding my hand back to where it had been, except now there was this other texture. He moved over me, and I opened my legs, impatient to bring him closer but wary of the column starting to push starting to push against my flesh.

How was it going to get inside? Nothing thicker than a tampon had penetrated before.

Felix had been kissing my neck and my breasts. Now he hunched down, and I felt his tongue sliding between my labia, drumming lightly, teasing. Impatient, I pulled his head up, back up to my mouth, and pushed my hips up against him. There was that pressure again, deeper now, a little way into me and painful.

"You're very tight," he said. "I don't want to hurt you." I wrapped my legs around him, wanting him to persist, brave, determined – hungry. They were strong dancer's legs, but he kissed me on the forehead and pulled away, and rolled over on his back. Panting, he said, "No big deal. Sometimes it takes a while."

I was furious.

"For Christ's sake, I'm not a china doll. Stop treating me like I'm a child. I told you yes."

"It's not a contest," he said. "This is meant to be pleasure for both of us, and – hey, I'm sorry – I just haven't had much experience with virgins." He turned on the desk lamp and I saw him frowning at me. Or puzzled. Whatever, his attitude enraged me. The Cheshire Cat was scowling down at me too, clearly implying: *This is what happens to girls who're too easy.* I'd wanted him too much.

"Maybe this wasn't such a good idea. Maybe I'm just not your type, whatever the hell that is." I wriggled off the end of the bed, retrieving panties and bra.

"Sally, please don't leave."

But I put on my dress, struggling with the zipper.

"Wait. If you want to go, I'll walk you home."

"No. I don't need you to. I'll be fine on my own."

"Then go!" he said and turned away. I stomped out, almost bumping into Mrs. Buchowsky. She was carrying a birthday cake and smiling benignly.

"Hello, dear! Are you a friend of Felix's? I was just bringing him a little something special." I mumbled an apology and slipped past her, out the back door and down the path, wondering if he'd managed to cover up before she walked in on him. I strode back to campus in the dark, sniffing back tears, and hoping he was embarrassed.

Lights were still on in the music department. I found an empty practice room and started pounding through scale after scale on the piano, doing my best not to think, not to feel, seething. I was a fool, and got what I deserved — but he was more of one. *Idiot! He's supposed to be such a man of the world. Are we over?* And fixating on one question: *Am I still a virgin?*

Finally, lying on my back in the narrow dorm bed, staring up at the ceiling with the network of shadows cast by the tree outside, I started to relax. It was only then, as I drifted into sleep, that I remembered his words: "Then go!" and somewhere deep inside heard the hurt in his voice. He was a boy after all.

~ 4 ~

Pockets

The Salvation Army is coming to take four big bags of
Felix's clothes. I considered selling some through the
local second-hand store. Money is tight until I can sort out a
separation of our affairs, and I could do with the cash. And
risk seeing his stuff on other people? That would be
unbearable. Rather let it go somewhere far away.

I've consulted with his kids, Joanie and Trevor, and
promised to send them the items they requested. They are half-
siblings but close, both in California, and probably not about
to come visit now that their father is gone. We've had such
wonderful times with them, excursions to the Namibian desert,
days of hiking through the green ravines of the Garden Route,

stuff I'd never done before. And without them, probably never will do again.

Each in their way has sought to console me and claimed they are fine, that they've known for years this could happen, that he could go suddenly, without saying goodbye. They have also been far away from him for so long, what does this change?

"I always talked to him in my head – arguing with him usually," Joanie said, her voice cracking. "Why can't I just carry on doing that?"

I know she would find comfort in a talisman, something concrete to clutch when his absence seems too abstract to accept. I put to one side, among other things, the small black case with the compass Felix claimed he used on his travels. It's elaborate, with a gold rim – a gift, he said, from an emir who befriended him in a bazaar in Oman. She is an avid wilderness hiker, and maybe she will actually use this. I know she'll treasure it.

Trevor asked for Felix's old leather bomber jacket. That's hard. I don't want to part with it. That thing was like his second skin. It has badges and patches and scrape marks that tell more than his journals. But this son also sees it as part of his father's identity, and I promised to send it soon.

In preparation, I go through the pockets, before folding the jacket and placing it in a fabric wrap that will protect it from the plastic bag that will go into the padded envelope. What a palaver, maybe more than necessary, but it's how I think it should be done. There's a traffic ticket in the breast pocket. Paid? Probably not – but it's from two years ago, and I discard it before I can start worrying about whether it should be paid anyway. He drove – and rode – so fast, I'd be surprised if there weren't more of those.

The left pocket is empty, except for a scrap of notepaper with a scratched-out doodle for a gadget of some kind. He always had ideas brewing, and there are pieces like this all over the house

In the right pocket I find half a tube of salty licorice pastilles. He loved those. I can't stand them. Leave them in there? No, they might get sticky in transit and cause problems. Into the garbage, though it hurts because I can see him absent-mindedly reaching in to get one, and chewing as he worked on his latest motorcycle, or strode along the shore path.

In the inside breast pocket my fingers encounter something rectangular and metallic. I take out a small harmonica that was a gift from me, and deep in my aural memory I hear an echo of "Softly, As I Leave You."

Student Felix played it just well enough to make the song recognizable, staring at me as he blew up and down that little instrument. I don't think he knew the lyrics, but he told me they were written by a South African guy, which we thought was very cool. I looked him up; it was true – someone called Hal Shaper had adapted an Italian song. Sinatra had sung it, and Elvis. Every time Felix played it, I felt like crying.

He was taught to play the harmonica, he told me, by a girl he shacked up with in Paris in early '66. He knew exactly when and for how long. I tried not to remember the details. She also taught him certain techniques not usually known to well-brought-up daughters from strict Catholic families. Not ones from Polish-Jewish families either. I shiver with pleasure remembering the long-ago tickle of his warm breath playing up and down me.

This afternoon, in the drawer where we've always stashed the coffee filters, I come across a crumpled envelope with 500 Rands in it. Unlike Felix to leave cash lying around, but very welcome, just enough for groceries for the rest of the month if I'm careful. By then, I should have dealt with the damn bureaucracy and sorted out my cash flow.

Thank you, my sweetheart.

But just when I'm contrite and trying to be sensible, another real estate agent calls. She used Felix's cell phone number. I haven't heard it ring in weeks and scramble to find it under a pile of unread newspapers. Surprised the battery is still working until I remember plugging it in to recharge, an automatic action.

"No, Dr. Barnard isn't here," I snarl at this woman. "He's dead, though his battery isn't."

Will I save money if I discontinue his number? It occurs to me to look through his old text messages, to see who was communicating with him. Sheepish, but still tapping through the names. There are a few familiar ones, and a couple I don't know. Like worrying a loose tooth, I'm probing for pain.

The paranoia is worst in the dark hours of trying to sleep, feeling abandoned in our semi-empty bed. Usually I can halt the spiral in the clear light of day, but now up pops an "Isabelle" who says she's been trying to reach him. The name rings a bell but my fuzzy brain won't yield recognition. Who the hell is she?

If I could just have him back... But, with these sickening

doubts, would I want that? Stupid question. Of course, of course, I would have him back any which way, with whatever faults — just for one more hard, hot hug. My arms feel lame these days, embracing nothing but garbage bags.

Right now, however, my biceps are still recovering from plastering yesterday. A stain the shape of a gargoyle had appeared on the sloping ceiling of the attic, probably from a leak in the roof. Not sure what the right method is, but the agent's visit prodded me into attempting a quick cosmetic job. I felt like Michelangelo, straining upwards like that, and I think I did a masterful job. The labor stilled my mind.

Sprawled on a deck chair, I rub the muscles and gnaw on a rusk, watching how fast the clouds scud across my field of vision. And then the stupid question intrudes again: Who the hell is Isabelle? I give a grunt of disgust and disturb the wagtail bobbing about near my feet, retrieving the crumbs I let drop. It flits into a bush, but when I'm silent, it comes back. I know I should know who Isabelle is, and the failure is infuriating.

Busyness should help. I go back inside and start vacuuming briskly around the furniture, back and forth. An hour of cleaning is all I can handle. I settle in the spare room and give myself what has become my treat, a brief escape into the beloved space of Felix's mind.

Reading bits and pieces of the "#3, 1965, India" volume. Each notebook seems to start with the country named on the spine and go on to surrounding places. Hence, this one includes jaunts in Pakistan and Nepal and stretches spent in various meditation centers and retreats. When did the Beatles do their Indian mysticism thing? Felix was ahead of the curve, venturing into experiences that are common now but were exotically strange back then.

Money was a problem. He got by with odd jobs, good luck, and the kindness of strangers even poorer than he was. *"I thought the poverty in SA was bad but somehow this seems worse. Or am I just seeing up close what was always at a distance at home?"* he wrote. The filth in Calcutta and the lack of Western plumbing where he stayed in Kathmandu — so much of what he described would have sent me hunting for the first American Express office, urging my parents to wire me money so I could book a flight home. Felix wasn't perturbed — except by one aspect, the passing of time.

"I'm getting older with nothing to show for it," he wrote at a hostel in the rugged mountains of Pakistan. Ironic, given he was only twenty-two. But we only know ourselves as older than we were, not as younger than we're going to be.

> *"People here are so calm. Just accept their lot in life. I can't be like that. I'm trying. I do my morning practice. For a while I'm peaceful – till I see another kid scooting along on his bum in the dust because his legs don't work and I get mad. Or you see a man begging because his hands are twisted and he can't work.*
>
> *All these months are passing and I'm just a parasite, contributing nothing. I wish John would come see for himself. These are the problems he should be attacking, not making his crazy products no one needs."*

There's another of those scratched-out patches, a line or two of something he wrote and then blocked out. This time I can't make out anything except "*I wish, wish, wish J...*" If there was a girl he broke his heart over, he never gave any indication of it. The Felix I met seemed impervious to heartbreak. Or maybe it was something to do with Mr. Latimer and that desire to inspire the inventor to take action.

Felix's mentor is still alive. Looking at the mementoes on display in this room — small-scale prototypes of two Latimer contraptions, framed certificates, artifacts from exotic locales — I start wondering about the old guy. He is in a retirement home on the other side of the mountain, in Camps Bay. Felix and I would go visit him every few weeks. When I called to tell him Felix was gone, he took it quite philosophically, as the very old do, as if he expects to see him quite soon on that other plane. But he did ask plaintively if I will still come to see him.

Felix had so little money at Rhodes. He kept track of every cent, even the cash he gave to the beggar who was a permanent fixture at the entrance to the campus. Was it John who helped? I didn't ask. In my family, finance questions were considered no-go territory, strictly private. But suddenly it's obvious. I know John urged Felix to do a degree, sent him money in Europe, and later helped him find work in some cutting-edge labs. No wonder Felix and wife Number One named Joanie in his honor. I feel a wave of gratitude to him too. I will go visit when I'm ready to venture out again.

The realization about John is satisfying. I feel like a forensic musicologist, those people who solve the who-when-why mysteries of the music world. Maybe that should be my next professional chapter. If I can slice through Felix's brambles, I can solve anything.

Dusting the brass and amber resin hourglass that stands on top of a file cabinet, another mystery calls for attention: Felix's fixation with time. Perhaps he sensed how abruptly his own portion would be cut short. When we were students, he always knew how many weeks were left in a semester and how old his heroes were when they died. He'd spout data on how long it took for trees to grow, or the body to renew its cells. I have no idea where that began, but it is underlined by the stash of calendars I find in that filing cabinet. Large and small, illustrated and plain, most marked with notes and reminders, and they go back decades. They seem to have become his substitute journals. Do I keep them? Read through them? Toss them? Burn them?

Picking out some at random, I notice a similar scribble next to various dates. Drawing was not one of this guy's talents but I work out that the vertical arrow with a halo of dashes represents a candle. Birthday notations? I see "JB" — or is it "JL"? — next to July 15 each year. John Latimer? No, it's definitely a B.

His own birthdays, of course, get no mention. But I find mine marked in '73 and '77, and '80, all years when we had no contact. A wave of warmth like from a slug of whisky rises when I see a query next to June 23, 1977: "*Can S be 30?!*" Across that huge divide, he was tracking my time too. Hugging that notion, I get shoes on, and walk down to the main street, to a spot where I can watch the fishing boats nosing their way in from the choppy ocean to the smoother waters of the harbor.

∽

We came very close to losing one another right near the beginning, in March of 1968. I wish there was a record of what happened on his side, but the calendar notations began later, and I remember now the last date I've seen on his journals is 1967, the previous year, on the spine of #5.

Through the next two weeks after his birthday, Felix didn't come by the dorm, or call, or come sit with me in Physio. If our eyes met in class, we nodded a greeting and looked away. It ached like a deep bruise.

I'd told Angie and Bev that Felix and I had a fight and weren't seeing each other anymore. I didn't go into the details, and they left it at that. They were used to me being the shoulder to cry on and not having much juicy stuff of my own to share. Bev was always drowning in work and too beleaguered to worry about me. Thinking back, I guess she had attention deficit disorder, but she called herself an airhead, and I went along with that, loving her anyway. She loved me back with earnest loyalty. Angie was a different case, smart as a whip and very funny, taught by an alcoholic mother that sarcasm was her best defense. She could have used it on me, challenged me to pull myself together, but for once she didn't.

Way more than usual, I hung out in the common room while the others played their beloved rock records. I can still hear them – "Sunshine of Your Love," "Light my Fire," "The Sounds of Silence." The lyrics resonated. Through my silence, they linked me to the world of forlorn lovers. Never a nervous eater, I found myself eyeing other people's candy, even their cigarettes, wanting concrete sensations to block the formless ones roiling inside. Angie offered to find some marijuana. Said she knew someone who knew someone. I said no. Only the real weirdoes on campus were getting high back then, and it was a sure-fire way to get kicked out of the dorm. I wasn't that desperate.

One thing went well – my writing. The poem I handed in to my English professor impressed him so much he waited for me after his next class, waylaying me as we all came tromping down the stairs of the lecture hall.

"Miss Paddington, what happened?" I shrugged, confused. "You've always been a good student, diligent and quite insightful, but I wouldn't have pegged you as the creative type. But this was truly impressive. You moved me, my dear, and that's something I can rarely say these days. I hope to see more work of this caliber."

Praise was all very well, but I hoped he wouldn't see more, not if it cost this dearly. The theme he'd assigned was "Nature, with a ballad," and what flooded my mind was a landscape stripped bare of vegetation, its skeletal convolutions battered by wind and icy rain. I was a doomed maiden loitering lovelorn on the moors. Purple poetry perhaps, but that image dogged my dreams for nights afterwards.

Help came from a totally unexpected source – Felicity, the blond bitch who'd tittered as Felix and I went off to our first coffee encounter. Her room was closest to our only phone so she was most often the person who answered it, yelling down the hallway for whoever was wanted. As senior student, I'd asked her to do it more quietly – maybe go knock on the door, but the system worked, and she got a kick out of knowing everyone's business.

She noticed I wasn't getting any calls from my "bad boy." As lunch was ending the second Thursday after our split, she slipped into the vacated chair next to me, flicked back her Jackie Onassis pageboy, and said, "Bunnington, I'm worried about you. Is everything all right?" To my horror, I burst into tears over my half-finished shepherd's pie. Angie and Bev both looked up in astonishment and hurried over to comfort me, but she blocked them with her shoulder. I was her project.

"Did that bad boy of yours hurt you?" she asked. "You're uptight, but you're pretty enough that you shouldn't have to put up with bad treatment. I thought he looked like a bastard the first time I saw him."

Another day, I might have pointed out no one deserves bad treatment, regardless of their looks, but I was too miserable. "He's not a bastard," I whimpered. "He didn't mean to hurt me. I hurt him. I was stupid."

She grasped my shoulders and squawked at me, "Well, in that case, what the hell are you doing mooning around here? Go tell him you're sorry."

It was pouring. I had an essay due the next morning, and my mother would be phoning later for our regular Thursday check-in. But I put on my boots and my raincoat and borrowed Felicity's umbrella. I splashed up the street to the Buchowskys', worrying all the way that it might be too late.

It was the first time – and maybe the only time ever – that I swallowed my pride and took the initiative to make peace.

The back door was locked and there was no bell, so reluctantly, I went around to the front. The maid answered, closely followed by Mrs. B, who led me through the house to

Felix's room. She stopped me before I could knock and whispered, her face stern, "He's a sweet boy normally, but he's been like a lion with a thorn in its paw. I don't know what you did to him, young lady, but you should make it right," and off she stomped.

As if I wasn't scared enough. Was he too angry to take me back? I almost turned to follow her, but he opened the door and I flung my arms around him before he could say anything. There was a moment of stiffness – surprise? – and then he gave a great whooshing sigh and engulfed me, whispering, "Oh, my sweet girl, my sweet girl."

No self-consciousness this time. Barely enough delay to put on a condom. And if there was pain, I didn't notice it. I just wanted him in as deep as he could go, all the way up to my heart. I didn't even register the hard knot of hair pressing against my head until we calmed down afterwards, and then it was me who flung the pins aside.

"You know what the egg said to the chicken?" he asked me, trailing finger tips across the thigh I'd flung across his belly. "They're lying in bed, you know – after, and the chicken lights up a cigarette..."

"No. What did the egg say?"

"Actually, the punch line is, 'Now we know the answer to that question,' but I don't think we solved it, did we? – unless you're a really good actress."

It took me a moment, and then I cackled. "'Who came first?' Just so you know, I'm hopeless at acting." He burst out laughing too and started kissing me again.

I felt like a cat full of cream. Hmm, were it not for the

condom... Now I was in on jokes like that. Bunnington melted. And head over heels in love.

~ 5 ~

Ladder

What am I going to do with myself? Getting out of bed feels like too much of a task this morning. I lie on my side of the bed, still unable to spread across the center, and wonder: *Once the house is sold and I'm settled somewhere, how will I justify my existence?* Emptiness looms ahead. How did a life so full and satisfying come to this?

I force myself to shower and dress in paint-spattered jeans and an orange sweatshirt that I stole from Felix because it looked silly on him and pretty good on me. He agreed.

The truth is, B.F. – before coming to live with him – I was turning into a social hermit. Libby, a pal from my graduate student days in Boston, was still in my life but always busy with her kids and now grandkids. Everyone had family except me. For a jarring moment, I'm nostalgic for the warm, rowdy gatherings with my ex-in-laws, the interplay of deep American voices as my husband Charles debated with his father, my sisters-in-law comparing recipes, the nieces and nephews nagging me to come play multi-hand piano jingles with them, Mom-Ethel watching us all with matriarchal pride.

I loved all that, and adapting to being single afterwards was an uphill struggle. The familiar pinch stings high in my nostrils when I imagine doing it again, being that "plus one" at Passover *seders* and Thanksgiving tables.

Who the hell is Isabelle, and what was he doing with her?

Forget that bullshit. I need to go up on the ladder to see what's happening with the roof. Jacob says there are loose tiles, and maybe some are missing. The source of the gargoyle stain? He has offered to do the repair but I'm scared he could get injured. I might have to call in a roofing company, but what will I do if they say a new roof is needed? I might not be the owner, but it's still my responsibility. I can't ignore it.

With conflicting images ricocheting in my head – of that blissful first lovemaking and suspicion about Felix's mystery caller – I drag the ladder out of the garage, balance it up against the side of the house, and teeter up, rung by rung. My sense of balance is generally excellent, but I've never done this before without someone standing at the bottom to keep it steady. As I move higher, the ladder creaks, complaining about the weight. I think about giving up and descending, but I'm already two-thirds of the way up and can almost make out the problem area.

How many times in my life have I had second thoughts, recognized folly but been too proud to admit it and extricate myself? Probably not the best moment for this introspection.

From up near the top, I can see over the neighbors' hedge. June and Zac's trio are playing in their sandbox. The little boy spots me and squeals in delight. His sisters wave, and I tentatively lift one hand to wave back.

Not smart. The vertical is lost. The next thing I know the whole scene is swaying wildly, and down I go, with a yodel that seems to come from someone else and ends in silence, echoing in my head.

Nothing hurts. I just can't breathe. Or see. Or remember how to move.

Vaguely, the thought occurs that this is bad. One's not meant to hit the ground that hard. And no one except the kids knows what happened. No one will come to my aid. There's warm liquid spreading against my cheek. If I'm bleeding, maybe this could be fatal. And I don't give a damn. It's kind of what I want.

Now I am seeing, and quite clearly: below me, a body in an orange sweatshirt, curled up on her side on the paving stones, with a trickle of bright red seeping out from under her halo of white hair. Serenely, the fact registers — that I am up here observing my body down there. What a sorry sight!

Then through the gap in the hedge comes June, dragged by the hand by her eldest, Samantha, who is shrieking, "Aunt Sally, Aunt Sally, please don't be dead! It's our fault, we made her fall!" And whoomp! I'm back in my heavy body on the ground, struggling to sit up.

Nothing is broken. Aside from a gash on my head and bruises everywhere, the wet-behind-the-ears young doctor can't confirm anything's wrong or find any excuse to keep me in the hospital. He dismisses me with a prescription for pain killers and an admonition to "Stay off ladders." Says to keep an eye on the bruises and check back in a week. A dire diagnosis might have meant sedation, being kept in bed, looked after.

As I'm slowly gathering up my bag and jacket, ready to walk out, he says, "The friend who brought you in mentioned you lost your husband quite recently."

"Not my husband," I reply, "but yes, recently."

"Are you sleeping? Would you like a little something to help knock you out? It's very important that you get a decent night's rest, and that can be hard when you're alone after many years with a companion. How long were you together?"

"Only five years." I glower at him, remembering that moment of thinking I was about to join Felix, and wanting to blame this character for bringing me back, though it had nothing to do with him.

"Ah, a mature romance? I've been trying to persuade my mother to try SeniorDate, even if it's just to find companions to go to concerts with," and he twinkles at me.

I want to say, "Fuck you! He was the love of my life – my whole life!" but am too tired and quivery to bark. Instead I just say, "We'd known each other nearly 50 years…"

The next morning, I wake up with my head throbbing and every segment of my body registering resistance. My back, especially, is rigid as a washboard. In a weird way it's welcome. For the first time in all these weeks the hurting is physical, not emotional. It's simpler. I glug down two pain killers, feed Mergatroid, make my coffee, and — tired all over again — hobble to the couch armed with another of Felix's journals, though I might be too woozy to concentrate. There was a single item on today's to-do list, sorting out that other box under the bed, the one filled with his old files. Maybe someone will shred them for me or put them in an incinerator. I'll work that out some other time.

The book falls open at a page headed "*Bombay. 7 August.*"

> "*Saw an amazing performance at a Hindu temple. The dancers were so lithe, it's like they have no bones. The music weaves and whines and their limbs move like beautiful snakes. Tried to talk to the women afterwards — but couldn't get anywhere near them. A huge bloke with a gray beard and a turban blocked the way. I suppose I'm not the only guy who fancies them. I wanted a dancer of my own to take home with me.*"

Damn you, Felix. A dancer did come to live with you and what did you do? You buggered off and left her.

I put the book aside and rise, a flickering spark of rebellion prodding my muscles into action. Standing in front of the French doors to the patio with my reflection fragmented by shadow and light, I hum my idea of an Indian tune. Slowly I lift my pale, soft arms above my head and, my feet in backless Turkish slippers, cautiously lift and step to the rhythm. It feels good to be moving, even with all the stiffness. Thankful no one else can see me, I dedicate this performance to the ghost swaying beside me, egging me on with an approving nod. A more ambitious sequence starts taking shape in my mind, with two or three dancers. I hobble in search of paper and pen to make notations before the image fades, excited and grumpy at the same time.

I lie down, panting. *Why did we take so long to come together?* That is a forbidden thought. Felix and I made a pact: We wouldn't waste any time on regrets or recrimination. I've tried so hard to honor it, but in all this silence, the question keeps seeping through, like that dampness on the attic ceiling. *We were so good for each other when we finally gave it a chance, so why the hell did we wait until it was almost too late?* I stand up again and start exercising very gingerly, stretching up and out and down, trying to loosen my joints and shove the bafflement back into oblivion.

The mood won't dispel. I'm angered by the finality. So many times Felix and I parted and I thought I'd never see him again, but each time I did. Why should this time be different? I punch the air, and it's a mistake. Now I hurt more.

The phone jangles and I collapse back on the couch, annoyed and depressed, and grab it from the side table, bumping my coffee cup as I do. A pale blob spreads across the black lacquered surface, and I try to mop it with a tissue as I answer.

"Are you OK? You sound real breathless." It's Joanie, California twang and all.

"I'm fine. What's up, my darling?"

"Can I come visit you? Eric wants to attend an architecture conference in Johannesburg, something about low-cost, green housing. He suggested I come too, get away from all the campaign nonsense here. He'll go off and do his thing, but I would so love to spend time in Kalk Bay, be with you. Do some mountain hikes. Be where Dad was."

Until she mentioned visiting, I hadn't registered how isolated I've been. Friends pop in, and they ask me out, but I've turned away most invitations. I'm still processing, I tell them. But to have this beloved girl here, even if just for a little while — the mere thought makes the room seem warmer. My aches begin to ebb.

"How soon are you planning to come?"

"Well, actually, real soon. Next week, if that's cool."

"You might be just in time to welcome Mergatroid's kittens." I'm hoping she'll also handle some of the choices I haven't been able to make, like what to do with the calendars and the shoes. And I'm hoping they will stay a while. Who knows if they'll ever come again.

I'm so energized, I go in search of Jacob, who's at work in the garden, carefully watering my parched plants. The winter rains haven't shown up yet after a very dry summer, and they need nurturing. The indigenous ones — the spiky strelitzias and the protea bush still dotted with the dried remnants of its pearly pink blooms — don't mind the neglect, but others do. I feel bad, but that doesn't matter right now.

He knows Joanie from her previous visits, and he shares my delight. Then he gets serious. "Madam, you must tell her she must be more careful. Last time she was here she was going to places that are not safe for a woman by herself. Master Felix, he didn't want to listen, to tell her no, but these days there are too many *skollies* around."

His concern is welcome – he speaks from experience, from his own run-ins with ruffians on the train and in the township where he lives. "Black-on-black violence" the American media would call it, as if that's somehow different than all the other opportunistic, poverty-driven crime the world over. I promise to pass on his warning.

He'd also reprimanded me for going up the ladder. I wasn't even going to tell him, but he noticed earlier that I was hobbling, and I had to confess. He shook his head from side to side, going, "Ai, ai, madam. Madam is not a young person. Master Felix, he would not have let you do that." Always that reference back to the real authority. Well, I learned my lesson, didn't I?

Talking of authority, another light goes on re Joanie. This is the one person who might have answers for me. I bet if I find the calendar from thirty-three years ago, Joanie's birth will be marked on it in huge, jubilant letters. She was her father's pride and joy.

"Having her and then Trevor," Felix told me a few years ago, "doubled my motivation and probably tripled my fear for the future, but it wiped out some of that ego nonsense about leaving a legacy. They are future enough for me." And then he remembered my situation, and apologized. He didn't need to. I'd come to love his kids almost as if they were my own flesh and blood.

We were in the kitchen making breakfast. He stole a crispy strip of turkey bacon from the pan, and paused, scrunching up his face. "Actually, they're not quite enough. I don't care about fame but I do want to know that my work has made a lasting difference. You feel that way too, don't you?" I shrugged. It was something I had wanted, but since coming to live with him that drive seemed to have seeped away into the reeds and weeds of daily life.

I still don't really care, or maybe I do — for both of us. Is all the expertise we gathered over all these years just going to disappear with us?

✍

Journal "#4, 1966, Japan." The handwriting is marginally better than usual, inspired perhaps by the beauty of the notebook. It's hand-sewn with an embroidered cloth cover. I skim over the mention of a long-limbed Danish girl Felix befriended for a few days and found remarkably agile and read instead of his encounter with three geishas at a tea house, "Rika, Riko, and Ruka." He was enchanted by their grace. There is a picture of them that comes loose as I open to that page, the glue dried by time, showing the coy smiles on their white-white faces. One has her hand over her mouth to hide the fact that someone has made her laugh. Typical Felix.

This page is followed by a very different passage describing his rage that so much manpower and wealth and human brilliance were being wasted on a crazy war.

> *"The Allies fucked up this country in World War II, and now there's the bullshit going on in Vietnam. We deserve to go extinct. Be better for the rest of creation. God made a huge bloody mistake with us. But...then look at Tokyo with all its crazy energy, and see the ancient temples, and watch these fantastic*

*people doing everything with such fucking amazing
precision, and they make me believe again."*

Good to see that youthful passion. Not that it mellowed
much; Old Felix was just as angry about America's war in Iraq,
and the waste of lives in the Syrian civil war, and in awe of the
Japanese again with the way they rallied after the tsunami in
2011 and the nuclear disaster at Fukushima. If he could have,
I think he'd have gone there to help.

Thank goodness he didn't. His own eruption, the first
aneurism, happened just a month later. Had he been in a hostel
somewhere or on a flight, he might not have survived. It burst
as he was working in the garden, trimming his prized protea
bush.

Edith and Roxanne, walking by with their dogs, saw him
fall. "I screamed, and you know I'm not the screaming type,"
Roxie told me, thinking back. "Edith ran for our friend Dr.
Webster, who lived next door. I got out my mobile and called
for an ambulance. We were frantic. But the dogs were strange.
You know how yappy they can be, but they went very quiet.
They just leaned against him as if to keep him warm."

Felix told me he heard their voices but couldn't move, not
even his eyelids. Recalling that now, after my own episode, I
can empathize in a totally new way with a fresh question: Did
he also have the floating-above, out-of-body experience? He
wasn't into spiritual stuff and he said no such thing, but that
might have made him rethink his atheism. It's shaken mine, or
at least my notion of an existence that survives the physical
plane. I want to believe there is a dimension where we might
reunite.

He felt the heat from the dogs' bodies. "They were like an anchor keeping me present, keeping me here," he said.

If the four of them — women and dogs — had not come by right then… The thought is unbearable. If I had received the news that he was gone, though we hadn't met face-to-face in a long time, my world would have cracked in half.

On the other hand, were it not for that crisis, I probably would not be here. Likely, I'd still be ensconced in my little lair in Brooklyn, taking courses in positive thinking in between giving courses in how to teach dancing. Were it not for — fate? the gods? God? the dogs? — intervening.

It's cold up here in the attic in the afternoon. Even in the summer, the sun dips behind the mountain before mid-afternoon, so the whole house cools down. The autumn sun only reaches through these windows in the morning, across the pearly spread of False Bay. Despite my sweater, I'm chilled, but I've got a bee in my bonnet about Felix's photos and he has boxes and boxes of them up here. He was such a record-keeper, I'm sure there are more images of where he went and what he did and who he did it with.

With no idea what I'm looking for, I brave the disconcertingly rickety stairs, more nervous about climbing than before but needing to be up here, with this soul-soothing vista. Not sure which creaked louder, them or me. They should be fixed. I'm pretty handy with a hammer, better than Felix was, but since my tumble, I'm loath to work too far off the ground, even indoors. I'll get over it, but for now it seems wiser to get in a skilled carpenter. Bite the bullet and pay for this one, before prospective buyers start traipsing through the house, lest any of them take a plunge.

The view from up here is glorious even through the dimpled panes. I haven't really appreciated it before. He was the one who climbed up, bearing stuff we didn't need but he wouldn't agree to discard. The space is jammed and awkward to navigate, but I feel embraced by his accumulated paraphernalia. More and more, I feel at peace up here. The quiet is punctuated only by the periodic "rr-whoosh" of the trains that run along the ocean's edge.

Mergatroid comes in search of me, demanding strokes and apparently accustomed to being up here. I hold her rounded, rumbly body for a while, and then, deep breath, put her down and tackle the pictures. Some are in albums, but most are stacked in boxes, methodically labeled like Felix's journals, with place names and dates. Were his handwriting clearer, it would be easy to track everything.

There are faded Polaroids and brown-tinged Kodak color snaps from Cape Town and his travels and from Rhodes, and clearer shots from more recent decades, with birthday candles lighting up faces that are vaguely familiar – wife Number One, Deidre? In-laws? Wife Number Two, Nellie? His kids. Felix isn't in many; most often, I expect, he was behind the lens, the record-keeper. But here and there I spot him, always with his arm around someone and wearing that knowing tiger grin. I can't not smile back at him.

Dipping in at random, different shots of Maria pop up. Thanks to that photo from the Barcelona bar, I now recognize her and enjoy her beaming smile.

"She's been a true friend," Felix said once.

I wasn't a true friend? "You? You've been the bane of my life," he replied.

I pushed aside my curiosity about Maria and the others. Being the new Sally and reveling in his way of being instead of trying to change him. This guy would talk to anyone and everyone, but he didn't talk about people, not in the gossipy sense. He would never speculate about them.

I'm the one who does that. Roxie remarked on it within weeks of meeting me. Leaning back with her fingers laced behind her head, she said, "I see you, always observing. You're fascinated by people, aren't you? But so covert! Why don't you come out with it and ask what you want to know?" She's a retired shrink and very sure of her own observations.

"My mother taught me it is not polite to pry," I claimed. She waved that aside and I couldn't deny her point. Right then I'd been wondering how on earth the two of them got together, Edith in her garden party florals, Roxie always in khaki pants and golf shirts.

"Go ahead, ask!" Edith said. They were devoted to Felix, and I was relieved they had welcomed me so warmly into their circle. We'd become genuinely fond of one another, and I didn't want to endanger that harmony. But this was license to ask, and with glee they proceeded to tell me their story. There was lots of chuckling over the shockwaves they caused in their respective families, but the humor didn't hide the hell they went through. Being openly gay in the South Africa of their youth took serious courage.

"And a very thick skin," Roxie declared, poking a finger in Edith's ribs.

"Ha, look who's talking. You never listen to anyone anyway," she replied.

By contrast, Felix and I had it easy. Our problems were all self-inflicted.

I should consult with Roxie and Edith about doing a memorial or a wake or something. They are very conventional in their way and devout fans of the good reverend, so they've probably nattered with him about my reluctance to deal with the issue. Personally, I fancy climbing on a burning pyre to express my devotion – but it's too late for that. Felix has already gone up in smoke.

~ 6 ~

Pictures

Among the photos, I find a picture of Felix and Maria on a beach somewhere, and another where they're huddled on a bench, bundled up in winter coats and scarves. *"How is it happening that two worshippers of sun are landing up in this very freezing Zurich?"* she had written on the back.

I'm not familiar with her handwriting but I know her brand of English. She and I have exchanged many emails and phone calls. After the kids and Roxie, she was the first person I called that morning of Felix's demise, to tell her and to say a long overdue thank you. It was she who brought us together.

Her voice clogged with tears, she stammered, "No, thank you, dear Sally, for how you were looking after our boy.

Without you, I am sure this would have been happening much sooner. He didn't look after himself."

She's invited me to stay with her if I go to Europe. Of course, though I think I've become more forthcoming, I haven't asked why she didn't come out to South Africa when she thought Felix needed help, and doesn't want to come now. I'd like to meet her. Of all the women in his life, other than Joanie, she is the one he mentioned most warmly — but even her he didn't discuss at length. All I know is that she did get married at some point, and their friendship continued. But then his and mine also survived our respective marriages.

In a box labeled "Rhodes," I find a 6-by-4-inch shot of Felix graduating, in a rented black gown and mortar board, me at his side. There's another later one, in an envelope, an official shot from Stanford University — of him with the striped band across his chest, and "Dr. Felix Barnard" printed below it.

On a framed corkboard I retrieve from my stock of teaching materials, I begin arranging some photos. It feels odd; I'm taking unaccustomed liberties with Felix's stuff. I know exactly what he'd say: "I don't care about that, but the light will fade those pictures." But I want these images visible where I can review them, if only for a while.

There are so few photos of him and me. But then, scrabbling through a box, I find a shot that halts me in my tracks. I knew it would be here somewhere, me with the three people I have loved best in the world: Felix in a jacket and tie for once; my mother, her hair almost as red as mine thanks to her hairdresser, beaming her best social smile; and my father, serious as always, impatient to be done with posing.

Pleasure and pain braid together like a challah loaf. Less than an hour after that picture was taken, Felix and I had one of our worst fights ever. It pitted us against each other like born enemies. Perhaps it foreshadowed the conflicts that came later, but if I was to go back and referee that clash, I'd tell those young idiots they were just opposite sides of the same coin. The more I brush sand off these unearthed fragments, the more that similarity is emerging, but it puzzles me. I know what I feared, but what made him so wary?

That evening came towards the end of our first year together, my last as a student. Just before the final exams, my folks called to say they would be traveling through Grahamstown on their way back from visiting friends in Durban. It would be their first meeting with Felix. "How about we take you and your Felix out for a fancy dinner?" my mother asked.

They knew about my boyfriend of course, though not in much detail — basically that he was an older student finishing the B.Sc. he had started by correspondence and that he wanted to work in medical research. They'd asked about his family because that's what they did with everyone: "Where are they from? What does his father do? How many siblings does he have?" My answers weren't satisfactory. The truth was, even after all this time, he had told me so little that I wasn't sure of the details, even the sibling question. He'd mentioned a younger sister, but two names had cropped up in passing. When I probed, he said he didn't like talking about his family and changed the subject.

We had a perfectly pleasant meal with Pops and Imma at

the best restaurant in town. It was in a pseudo Tudor building, and the décor equally pseudo but very cozy, centered around a giant fireplace lined on either side with copper utensils. Felix entertained them with discreetly edited stories of his travels, and I could tell they were impressed with his intelligence. My father commented approvingly on the passion he expressed for his work. "This boy will go far," he said in his professorial way.

Pops viewed the world with such deep caution, that vote of confidence almost made me cry. They say girls go for boys who remind them of their fathers. It wasn't true for me; Felix was everything my father wasn't – bold and sensual and optimistic. I think that contrast was half the attraction. But they did share a commitment to truth.

And Pops also saw something else. In a moment when my mother was bending Felix's ear with one of her own stories, he whispered to me, "Be careful with him, *meidele*. He is made of heroic stuff, but heroes also can be hurt. I am sensing a deep wound in this Felix of yours."

Imma, dressed to the nines in a satiny floral dress that made her bountiful bosom look even more impressive than usual, also watched him cautiously as she nibbled her way through the hors d'oeuvres. She softened as we got to the meat course. By dessert, she was recommending what he should order, patting his hand and bobbing her head in delight as he teased her. They were sorry he wasn't Jewish – even tried inquiring about his grandparents' names with the notion that he had Yiddish roots – but they cared much more that he was a *mensch*.

When he was out of earshot, Imma said, "Do you…? Are

you…?"

I knew exactly what she wanted to ask. It rasped against my own doubts. Did we have plans for the future? Were we sleeping together? Were we serious? With my voice lowered, I went into full brat mode. I hissed, "What business is it of yours? Just because you gave birth to me doesn't mean my body belongs to you." These days, I suppose, we might have argued about boundaries. All I knew then was that I had to repel her intrusion.

Felix came back just in time to catch my last words. His eyes narrowed. He sat down beside me and whispered, "Sally, how can you talk to her like that? She cares about you. Don't you get that?"

His reprimand made me steam even more. Of course, I knew she wanted me to be happy, just as much as my father did. What Felix didn't grasp was how much they wanted to see me settle down and get married. They wanted grandchildren – for themselves and always also for that other reason, to make up for the loved ones lost to Hitler. I wanted to demand who the hell he thought he was, querying my behavior. After all, it's not like he'd ever expressed interest in making an honest woman of me.

As we waved goodbye to them and started walking back to the dorm, I said, "How about we go to Port Elizabeth next weekend?" It was part revenge and part honest frustration, a desire to find out where he came from and maybe what I could expect from him in the future.

"How?" he asked. "And why?"

"On your motorbike. So I can meet your parents."

The bike bit added a second layer of anger I hadn't intended. In all the time we'd been going out, he had never agreed to take me on his Harley. In the beginning, I was cautious and didn't want to nag. But the more I saw him roar up to lectures on the bike, or arrive at the dorm to take me out and leave it parked outside, the more I wanted to try. I asked and then I whined. But Felix wouldn't hear of it, even when I offered to buy my own crash helmet. He simply wouldn't discuss the possibility.

He'd been equally dismissive about my meeting his family. "They're not your kind," he said now. "Take it from me, Sally. You think the boys here are chauvinists? You should see my brothers. They used to be Neanderthals and now they're worse. They're racist and ignorant and a waste of time. As for my father..."

"And you're arrogant," I hissed. I couldn't believe he was accusing me of being uncaring. I knew very clearly where I belonged on the morality scale. The muggy night air was making my hair frizz, and for once I didn't care. It blocked my view of him.

The street was deserted, but I kept my voice low. "You lecture me but you don't give a damn about your own mother. All you care about is Felix Barnard. If you wanted to, you could make peace with her – and probably with your father."

We had stopped in front of a brightly lit store window with a display of cleaning products. The neon gave Felix's face a blue tinge. "I care about my mother," he said. "I care more than you'll ever know."

"You've got a strange way of showing it," I shot back.

"I have no choice," he yelled. "My father won't let me in the house and my mother's got no backbone." I told him to hush before someone called the police on us for disturbing the peace. He lowered his voice but got even angrier. "I like that you stand up for yourself, but you're spoilt, Sally Paddington. You think life's a nice little stage play that has to follow your script. Well, it might work for you, Miss Perfect, but not all of us have parents who think the sun shines out of our arses."

We didn't kiss goodbye that night, and I didn't see him for days. Things didn't warm up again until we started writing exams. My first final went badly and apparently he nearly blew his too. We crossed paths at the cafeteria, recognized the look of misery in each other, and headed straight back to the Buchowskys'.

"Orgasm therapy," he called it. Sex made Felix happy. Sex with him made me happy too. We apologized to each other for the row and promised to be more understanding. I was heading back to Cape Town for the summer vacation. He was going to Namibia on a research project with his biology professor. I wanted every moment of closeness we could get. He did too.

~ 7 ~

Talisman

Of course, if sex united us, it also divided us. And now here I sit, in this cottage where we found happiness, and arrayed all around me are reminders of what linked us and what separated us. I have three items in my lap: an address book from goodness knows when stuffed with additional slips of paper, a postcard from Maria – one of many, and the little harmonica. They are props from our long pas de deux.

"Mixing our metaphors, are we?" my editor would have said. In New York, I was a professional aspiring to high standards. Here, I'm descending into shoddy sentimentality. Is it because of old age or grief? Can't do much about either. I shake myself and start to rise from the chair, but suddenly I remember who Isabelle is. They say if the blanks fill in, you don't have Alzheimer's. Thank goodness for that.

She came to one of the first parties I attended here with Felix, a fundraiser at a restaurant overlooking the harbor. Some boats had been damaged in a storm, and we were trying to help the fishermen survive till repairs were done and they could get back to sea. The ending of apartheid has done nothing to make their lives easier, and most of them live very close to the bone.

The event was Felix's idea, and he held forth eloquently, microphone in hand, describing the hardship the fishermen faced. I noticed a curvy brunette in very high heels hanging on his every word. When he finished talking, she grabbed a plate of fried calamari from one of the waiters and brought it over to Felix with a coy, inviting gesture. He took one, thanked her with a smile, and turned to speak with someone else. She hovered at his elbow, chiming in on their discussion and clearly trying to get his attention.

I ruined Isabelle's plan quite calmly and deliberately. I'd like to think this was the new Sally at work, defending my turf instead of storming off in a huff. Passive aggressive? Maybe, but actually not all that passive – and pretty effective. As one of the hostesses for the gathering, it was my duty to make newcomers feel welcome, so I went over to do that. I introduced myself, gave Felix a big, fat kiss in passing, and led her off to meet some other people. They included, let me say in my defense, Stan, the rather dashing accountant who was helping us handle donations.

Over mugs of hot Milo later, doing a postmortem of the event, I told Felix what I'd done. He chuckled. He said he noticed her, felt good that she fancied an old geezer like him, but had no desire to fan that flame. "I've got my hands full with you," he said. "Why would I waste time with someone else?" That memory takes my anxiety level down a peg or two.

Which reminds me, Stan might be a good person to consult about my finances. He has integrity, and I appreciate that he deflected Isabelle. The last time we saw him he suggested the four of us get together for a sail on his catamaran. Come to think of it, that might be why she called Felix. She could have called me, of course, but never mind that now.

Feeling better, I push the items off my lap and leave them on the desk, all except the harmonica. That I keep with me, in my pocket. Later I will put it on the mantelpiece, where I can see it each time I walk past.

We were so young when I gave Felix that instrument. It was his birthday, the second one we celebrated together. I had graduated and found work in King William's Town, two hours away, while he finished his degree. On alternate weekends I came back to Grahamstown to teach a dance class, and when he could, he came through to me on his Harley. What he did on the weekends when we weren't together was a mystery. Even when I was there, he would disappear at times, be gone all day with no explanation. He brushed aside my questions, and I was too scared to persist. He worked like a fiend – had from the start, as if in a race against some deadline – but I suspected he still had time for other pleasures.

This is the end of the Sixties, remember, and even in South

Africa, with our cultural time-lag, possessiveness was frowned upon. I tried to be laid back, not nag, not pry. I didn't own him.

So much easier to be cool in our old age – till now. From this little coastal haven of ours he would still disappear without explanation, taking off on his Harley to goodness-knows-where. I'd wave goodbye as he trundled down the cobbled street revving his engine and vanished from view. But it no longer made me feel I disappeared too. I accepted that Felix needed to be alone sometimes and he'd be back soon enough, hungry and full of enthusiasm about what he'd seen.

That birthday night my roommate in King William's Town was out, a discreet kindness on her part. I made us the fanciest dinner I could concoct, heating soup with an immersion heater in a jug on the kitchen counter. A chicken was sizzling in a Dutch oven on the single hot plate, and I'd made a salad the way I knew he liked it, with ripped lettuce and skinny sticks of celery and carrot he could eat with his fingers. While the chicken cooked, we carried our mugs of soup to my little bedroom and set them on the bedside pedestal. He flicked through my records and put on the Elvis Presley song we'd both come to love, "Softly, As I Leave You" – and we danced for a moment, bodies sliding across one another, and then sat down side by side on my bed.

When he put down his empty soup mug, I reached under my pillow and took out the Christmas-cracker-shaped package. He tugged loose the gold ribbon, opened the red crinkle paper, and grinned. Right away he put the harmonica to his lips and began experimenting – drawing sound on the inhale as well as on the exhale.

"This is magical," he said. He put it down on the quilt and slowly, gently, began kissing me, leaning his weight in to ease me down. Involuntarily, my breast bone arched towards him, but I resisted. I could smell the chicken already beginning to burn, and I pulled him up with me and drew him to the kitchen. We would be back there on the bed soon enough.

✌

With my fingers curled around the little instrument in my pocket, sitting on our big bed, I hum the "Softly" words.

To my surprise, anger bubbles up. That didn't used to happen. The song had an achy sadness that made us want to dance very slow and close. I register for the very first time that it's not about a guy who's dying, as Elvis suggested. He's sneaking out while his long-time lover is sleeping. He doesn't want her to wake up and beg him to stay. The son-of-a-bitch!

I jump up. The usual wind has subsided, and nothing is rattling or creaking. In that silence, a new thought comes stomping to the fore, stopping me in my tracks: I never begged Felix to stay. I was way too proud. If he wanted to be with someone else, he should go, piss off.

Thinking mathematically, striving for objectivity, I mentally check off the fights I remember. Truth is, very few were about other girls. They were about silly differences of opinion between two pig-headed individualists — about money or politics or religion. (That early agreement about atheism hadn't lasted; I was going through a pro-tradition phase and had taken to attending Friday night services in the tiny

Grahamstown synagogue.) Felix let go of his anger easily; I didn't. But eventually I couldn't resist him and he knew it. If he got close enough, if I felt his warmth, my flesh would take on a lightness, as if the cells were reaching for him whether my mind gave permission or not. Everything needed to press against him.

I'd find myself wanting to whisper, "I love you." I didn't because I knew he wouldn't. But he'd look deep into my eyes, as if reveling in my soul, and come up with something new he wanted to show me, some special corner of the botanical gardens, or a record he knew I'd adore, or a new and amazing discovery about human physiology.

But just as I'm trying to dismiss the subject of infidelity, a reminder punches me in the gut. I put to the side a photo of Felix and me next to his Harley, that big black bone of contention, and underneath it is a shot of Felicity, the dorm gossip, in an evening dress with her blond hair up in a beehive. "*For Felix from Felixity (haha), your biggest fan,*" it says on the back, with "*XXX*" and a heart. I start to rip up the picture and stop, forcing myself to face the memory.

Just as determinedly as she had helped us get back together the previous year, Felicity did her darnedest to break us up. It came to a head one Saturday, a few months after my move. I was back in Grahamstown to oversee a dance performance by township children at the big Anglican church on High Street.

Such an idiot! Here I am obsessing with the drama that followed, when the children's dance played a much more significant role in my future — and, against all odds, helped reconnect Felix and me.

But I'm not really a dance teacher anymore, and apparently I still am a jealous fool.

Our performance was part of a "town-and-gown" event to show local citizens how Rhodes students contributed to the community. These kids and their mothers had been working with me since my first year on campus, teaching me about Xhosa dance at a church hall in Fingo Village, the dirt-poor township that whites needed permission to enter. I taught them English country dances they found very funny. Even after leaving town, I'd come back twice a month to keep our little club in action – and spend the night with Felix.

We'd put together a "duel," with four kids doing the flat-foot, stomping Xhosa steps and four skipping through the English ones. Their show went off without a hitch, and the congregants were enchanted. The kids were beaming too, bubbling over with pride. I came away from it euphoric. My favorite, nine-year-old Winston – so super-talented – walked with me for a few blocks, holding my hand and chattering about how he was going to be a great dancer one day, like Rudolf Nureyev in the movie I'd showed them, flickering on a screen in the church social hall.

In that mood, I pranced up the path to Felix's place. I had hoped to see him at the church but wasn't surprised he couldn't make it. He was such a workaholic by then, and I knew he had a physics exam looming. And he hadn't promised. If he had promised, he'd have been there. Felix seldom gave his word, but if he did, he kept it.

I jab a pin through Felicity's beehive and tack the picture to the board. She had her part in our progression.

The outside door was open. As I approached his bedroom that Saturday, I heard water running in his bathroom. I knocked and when there was no response, I slipped inside, thinking I'd surprise him in the shower. He was standing in the middle of the room, naked, his penis at half-mast. It sagged. His face was a study in astonishment and something else. Not guilt. Pity?

"Oh, Copper Girl —"

I started to say, "You should have seen Winston. He was so wonderful. They all were...," when a voice piped up from the bathroom: "You coming, Felix? It's nice and hot, and we haven't got forever." The bitch herself. Hatred surged, all focused on her. I wanted to plow into the steam and claw her sticky blond hair.

He said, "Shit, today was your church dance day? I'm so sorry I missed it. Sally, please don't freak out about this. It's not a big deal."

I dumped the souvenir program on his desk and spun around, intending to storm out, but he grabbed my arm and pushed me onto the chair. "Wait!" he said. He hopped into his jeans and ducked into the bathroom.

I heard a shriek and "Why's she here?" and "Why should I go? Well, she's an idiot."

They came back into the room, Felicity wrapped in his blue towel, her hair dripping. It infuriated me that she was so tanned and tall. Even bedraggled, she looked glamorous. She scowled at me, snatched her clothes and returned to the bathroom. She called out from there, "You're a sucker for punishment, Bunnington. I told you way back he's a bastard."

I sat glaring out the window, kicking the leg of his desk, concocting revenge plots, until I heard the door close behind her. Then I turned and snarled at Felix, "If this isn't a big deal, how many other little deals are going on?"

He said, "Listen to me, these things happen. We didn't say anything about other people. I haven't asked you to live like a nun in King William's Town."

"Do you like her? — like really like her?"

He shrugged. "She's fun. She asked for help with math, and kept coming by to visit. We were horny."

I stormed out then and slammed the door so hard the bang reverberated.

It took a month before we made up. I was indignant and self-righteous, which drove him up the wall. He kept making his case for freedom — what people call "polyamory" now, plain old promiscuity then — and how humans are capable of caring for multiple lovers in different ways. That crap sent me into a tantrum every time. But Felix missed me, and finally he convinced me that he had foregone all others. His only condition was that I move back to town, which I wanted to do anyway. He suggested we get a place together, and all my resistance melted.

Flipping through his mountain of photos, I find them frustratingly uneven. So many about some chapters and so little about others. There's almost nothing to show for the months we lived together after my return in our tiny, one-bedroom apartment, the best we could afford on my salary as a teaching assistant back in the music department and what he got taking care of lab equipment. I loved it at first, just because it was ours.

No record of the deliciousness of our Sunday mornings, eating breakfast on the balcony, serenaded by the mixed choir of birds in the nearest jacaranda tree. Felix bare-chested in shorts, me in one of his shirts, both freshly showered and still flushed with pleasure.

Or the tension shared, dodging the police as we met with black activists from Fort Hare University, equally fired up to change the system though we had no idea how. Or the midnight swims in the dark water of the reservoir in the hills above the town, yelling as we hit the cold and gasping as we found each other's warm bodies. Or reading to each other in bed from books brought home for that purpose.

And there is no record of what went wrong, of the way claustrophobia began to grow as anger erupted between us over and over again. About what? His flirtations? His untidiness? My tidiness? My deepening suspicions about where he was when he wasn't with me?

No record of how the anger chilled into detachment, and the off-handed, couldn't-care-less suggestions — from him or me, bizarrely I don't remember who — that maybe we should "give it a break, see how things go." Arguments late at night when we were both exhausted, falling asleep back to back, not touching — and waking up still angry.

Careless, stupid youth, so cavalier with a gift — so unaware of how rare it is to find a bond like ours. If we'd only known. My chest tightens as I remember that terrible calendar page.

I'd been out all day, visiting friends in King William's Town, people Felix didn't know, and I strolled back into the apartment around sunset, wondering where he might be. It was instantly obvious: The place was echoingly empty. It even smelled different — more as it had when we moved in, of cement and paint rather than food and flowers. His books, his clothes, his pictures — everything was gone. I looked outside and, sure enough, no motorbike. And there was the note scrawled across November. The rest of the calendar was gone, with him.

How had I not seen it coming? He'd graduated cum laude, and job offers were coming in. There was vague talk about moving, about where we might live next, but nothing had been decided. It hadn't occurred to me that he might have accepted one of those offers. Was he planning to leave without me, or did he act on impulse? Right then, I hated him so much, I didn't care.

Did it really happen that way? Curled up in the threadbare old chair in the Kalk Bay attic, with his stuff all around me, I try to extract an explanation, but more and more these days I'm wary of what might be myth-making, tales I tell myself to make up for what the tide has washed away. And I know I've been seeking out cause for anger. Much as the bad stuff hurts, I want to rub it in. The burn helps nullify the hunger to hear his footfall, to see his face appear in the doorway, his warm hands reaching out to me.

I clamber up and go searching for I-don't-know-what, scrabbling through the pile of calendars. Way down I spot the purple crest of Rhodes University. There are three of them, 1968, 1969, and that year, 1970. Not much written on it beyond appointments and work deadlines. The note-making habit must have grown more intense over time. But I see the ragged edge of a missing page, and sure enough, it's between October and December.

The aloneness back then laps against the aloneness now, merging into a larger wave that swamps the anger. All I'm left with is this aching self-pity pressing against my rib cage.

~ *8* ~

Hats

Trudging along the sea road, I look down at the tangle of black seaweed covering the rocks exposed by the receding tide, and everything is ugly. If I lift my eyes, the expanse of grey-green ocean should be beautiful, but instead it's drab, like military colors. Beauty is fleeting, like passion, like happiness. We had plans, Felix and I, to build a pond in the garden, to travel around South Africa, to invite new friends for dinner. He has ruined all that.

The muscles in my calves keep knotting. I have to stop, rub them, and flex my feet before continuing. It feels to me as if all the stiffness comes from my back. A chiropractor might help, but how do you align energy that is all out of whack?

I breathe the pungent ocean breeze, the mix of rot and freshness. My hair whipping against my cheeks reminds me of his — long gray strands stroking my face as he kissed me right here, overlooking the rocks. I swipe mine away, irritated.

That December when he left me in Grahamstown, he became ugly in my memory. In retrospect his jokes were cruel. The way he walked around with just a towel around his hips was showing off. His dreams of creating medical miracles were arrogant, delusional.

Maybe all that was true. Maybe this whole lifelong adoration was ridiculous, a delusion.

But this is no one else's business. I'm coping. I try to convey that later to Rev. Someone Someone, the minister from the Presbyterian church, the one with sea winds blowing against its stained-glass windows but with a sheltered vestibule around the other side. I've only been there a couple of times, and not since Felix's departure.

I bump into him at the mini-mart, and he looks at me with such great pity, I want to punch him, dog-collar and all. There's the quick glance at my purchases. Why? — to see if I'm buying food or booze? He says he's concerned about me, that a couple of his parishioners have spoken of my isolation, and I should not bear my grief alone. *Reverend, are you offering to fill my empty bed?* Obviously, he's also concerned that there's been no funeral or memorial service for this man whom he'd come to regard as a friend, even if not exactly a member of his flock.

"Dr. Barnard and I had wonderful discussions," he tells me, putting down his own shopping basket, full of cans and frozen meals, and settling in to chat, though I have no such inclination. I witnessed some of those sessions, supplying snacks and ice to go with their whisky and then leaving him and Felix in peace. "We could argue about everything, from creation to the hereafter, without either one of us ever getting hot under the collar. I believe I speak for him as well as myself." He gives a little grin and tugs at his neck. "I doubt if I changed his thinking one iota, but I must admit he had some impact on mine here and there."

When I first arrived, he inquired about my religious leanings and my background. Felix informed him that I was "a fallen Jew, unrepentant and unredeemable." I heard him say to the minister, "I've never tried to convince her of anything, and I'd advise you not to try. My Sally had a mind of her own when I met her as a girl, and she's even more hard-headed now. That's what I like about her."

Couldn't he have used the other "L" word just this once? I'm a silly old bag, I know, but I still wanted to hear it – "love."

The fellow goes on about "closure," and I know he has a point. Finally, I ask him to give me a bit more time. "His daughter is coming. We can decide then what kind of ceremony we want."

Walking home, my mood darkens by the step. Saying goodbye to Felix isn't something I want to consider. *He didn't bloody well say goodbye to me.* Back in the cottage, I unpack my purchases, slamming them onto shelves. I'm never hungry these days but know I should make something, and usually cooking steadies my nerves. This time it doesn't help. Anger is tightening my throat as the heat rises from the stove.

Why this feeling? The thought of saying goodbye? Not

wanting to let go? Finally I hush the chatter and listen. Birds are squawking outside. In the distance a train gives its long, sonorous wail as it approaches the station. I go on preparing the food, trying to pin my attention to the color of the tomatoes and the crunch of celery, striving to feel grateful for this nourishment. Time will grind onwards.

Sitting outside, adequately fed and at a loss about what to do next, I start feeling angry about the other hollows in my life. I want to turn the clock back so that just a few miles away, in the shady suburb close to a different mountain, I can still find my parents. I want to find them in the living room with its floral lounge suite they bought with such pride, to snuggle into my father's flannel-suited arm, to feel my mother's cool hand on my hot cheek. Old as I am, I feel orphaned.

It's dangerous to play with time like this, to interrupt its normal linear mode, but the present is so unappealing, I feed into that chaos. Instead of following it like a train track from then to now and into the future, I let it fold back on itself, stalling around the horror dawn and buckling in the face of the total uncertainty ahead.

And thus back into the past, trying to recall what happened to that girl I was, and to Imma.

The first fright came in 1970. She was diagnosed with leukemia, and my world teetered. For all the fireworks between us, she was my North Star. Pops was even more lost. But she fought back. With each round, her wigs became more glamorous, and her fashion taste more gaudy.

I'd returned to Cape Town a few months after Felix vanished, rented a cottage, and gathered private music students.

Between them and working on my teaching diploma, I was getting by. I did some choreography for a children's dance company, and dated some nice enough guys, though nobody I could imagine marrying, despite my mother's wistful urging.

When the cancer returned a year later, I moved back in with her and Pops. He could not bear to see Imma in pain when there was nothing he could do to help. His solution was morphine. He wanted her sedated, anything that would remove her suffering. It was all I could do to convince him to stay away from her medications and leave them to me and the doctors. As she got better, he calmed down, and life again began to return to normal.

I saw Felix twice in those years, both times briefly.

The first was at a reunion in Grahamstown two years after we parted. I was shocked to see him. Nostalgic gatherings didn't seem like his thing. I was torn between wanting to turn and run — and wanting to run into his arms. There was no chance for either. Some woman was hovering at his side, and we were surrounded by other people. We exchanged a quick "How are you? It's good to see you," before being pulled away by friends.

I was waiting for a refill of ginger ale at the bar when he cornered me towards the end of the evening. He just said, "I owe you an apology."

I said, "Yes, you do. But it's ancient history. No hard feelings," trying to sound very offhand.

"Not so ancient. Twenty-three months ago," he began. One of his science buddies came bounding over, just as Bev appeared at my elbow, followed by Angie. I have no idea what he was going to say. When I looked again, he was disappearing into the crowd, and I was already running late to catch my ride back to the hotel. I tried to remember whom he'd been with, but just had the impression of someone brown-haired and clingy.

The following year, he looked me up on a brief visit to Cape Town and suggested we meet for dinner the night before he left. I was inclined to say no, but my mother overheard and insisted he come to the house. So we had dinner with her and Pops, and, to his delight, she made cold borscht and baked sweet apricot rugelach like she'd sent me at Rhodes. He was deeply concerned about Imma, and it cheered her to have his attention. He told us about his studies at the University of the Witwatersrand and his research into muscle regeneration, and he got my father talking about the way cultures rise and fall, doomed by their own success.

Apart from the pressure of his foot against mine under the table, we had no physical contact until I walked him to his motorbike, a shiny new Harley. It was cold outside, and I suggested we sit in my car.

To begin with, we just talked. Even after all that time, it pleased me to hear that he suffered too when we parted. I asked him why the hell he left the way he did, and he said I pushed him out, and we started arguing about whose fault it was. Neither had the heart to insist, and we agreed to differ, and went on to talk about our work and studies.

Inevitably, our eyes met, we leaned closer, and we started kissing. Hands were going everywhere, waking waves of desire in me. We joked that my parents might wonder why I was taking so long to come back inside, but we saw their bedroom light go out and stopped worrying about them.

It was delicious to taste his mouth on mine again, to smell that familiar muskiness, to feel his rough fingers slide gently along the scooped neck of my blouse. The car was tiny and we struggled to get closer. Felix found the handle that reclined the seats and leaned across me, murmuring words of desire, and then tried to clamber across to my side, but it was too awkward, with the gear stick protruding at just the wrong angle. I might have gone down on him, but the bedroom light came on again. There was a good chance my mother would come outside looking for me, and that was inhibition enough. We gave up, laughing and panting.

Even with the throbbing desire, I was glad, grateful for that interruption. Getting over him had taken so long, I didn't want the healing undone.

It would be a decade before we saw each other again.

~ 9 ~

Crossed Paths

How come I never realized how noisy Felix was as he went about his daily rituals? I miss the slip-slap of his bedroom slippers as he made his way to the bathroom, and the sound of him peeing and flushing and running his shower. He had given up closing doors, and I wasn't about to change his habits. Then he would slip-slap to the kitchen, call out a greeting to Mergatroid, and open the back door, humming all the while. The clink of coffee mugs would get me out of bed, eager to share that first mug with him. He would greet me with a "Good morning, my lovely one!" or "Hello, Copper Girl. How was your night?"

I hear his greeting in my mind and it pulls back another memory, a shockingly unexpected replay of those words. A cascade of feelings swirl around me, blocking out the eight o'clock news broadcast with its prattle about crime and the American elections. Happiness, regret, and guilt all intertwine.

It was early in 1983, when I was thirty-five. I went to Los Angeles to attend a huge conference on dance as therapy, to learn from others in the field and to give a presentation on my multi-cultural approach to dance education. I had developed that specialty from roots going back to those beautiful kids in Fingo Village, the ones who did their Xhosa/English duel at the church on High Street.

On a free morning during the third day of the conference, I found a seat in the sun on the palm-ringed deck of a restaurant in Hollywood and began checking my notes. With skin as pale as mine and the first bloom of youth starting to fade, I should probably have been in the shade, but those tables were taken and it was a blessed change after the months of New York winter. That morning especially I needed heat.

My move to the U.S. in 1977 had been thanks to Imma and my father. At their insistence, I accepted a scholarship to do a master's at the New England Conservatory in Boston. Not that I hadn't wanted it. Things in South Africa were tenser and more uncertain than ever, and the idea of fresh horizons was intoxicating. I'd lobbied hard to get the most glowing references I could from all my old professors and current supervisors and spent sleepless nights composing a sure-fire application essay. But then came the doubts. How on earth could I leave two people who had gone through so much loss in their lives, who loved me with such intensity, and enjoyed witnessing my daily life so much? But their love was selfless. It still knocks the wind out of me when I remember their generosity.

"You need a fresh start," my mother declared. "You need to find yourself a nice boy, and maybe get famous. How do they say in America? 'You can have it all.'"

She was well again after yet another round of chemo, but worried about the violence in South Africa. For all their sharp awareness of the injustice around them, she and Pops were petrified that one day black South Africans would rise to claim their rights and wreak revenge against all whites. The year before, in 1976, when the riots broke out in Soweto, their anxiety soared. Just the sight of smoke rising from fires in the distant townships tipped the scales: They wanted me out of danger, no matter what it cost them.

I went with my heart torn in two. So many people had been killed or jailed. My little dancer Winston, the star of the show at the church back in Grahamstown, was shot in the back, his mother told me in a letter asking for help. They didn't know if he would walk again, let alone dance. I sent money and the names of doctors in Port Elizabeth who offered to treat him, but the sense of helplessness was getting worse.

But somewhere in all the heartache was also a desire to escape from Felixland, as if new landscape could change the geography of the heart. My mother sensed that, I know.

At least once a week I wrote to her and Pops, including all the good news I could gather and mentioning any guy worth naming. Calls were so much more expensive back then, but they phoned faithfully on the first Sunday of every month, and we planned that I'd fly back once a year.

Home in Cape Town had been a cottage shadowed by oak trees, with the blue mountain in the distance. Now I shared a cramped third-floor apartment in Brookline, with a clanking heating system but great neighborhood coffee bars. Where transport had been my little white VW Beetle, getting places meant running for buses and trains and a lot of walking, often in snow. I froze my toes till I found the right footwear.

But it was all exciting and different. At last I was part of that wider world Felix had described to me. "After living on the far edge of cultural colonialism, where all our books and movies and music come from far away, it's like landing in the Promised Land," I wrote to Jenny, an old ballet school friend. While other foreign students waxed righteous about the U.S. role in Vietnam or the spread of consumerism, I blissed out on the arts. This was Louisa May Alcott and Robert Frost territory. The giants of dance and music whose theories I'd studied appeared in person to teach our courses or lead workshops.

Summing it up in an attempt to persuade Angie to also come study in Boston, I wrote, "Even on a bare-bones budget we could go hear the Boston Pops. I've seen dances created by Alvin Ailey and Bob Fosse, performed by dancers they worked with. I heard Bob Dylan perform live from so close I could hear him inhale!"

On the other hand, I was more of a misfit than ever. I didn't mention that to anyone back home. My new friends thought me well educated because of my Anglo accent – "Oh, you sound just like Mary Poppins!" – but not having grown up watching Saturday morning cartoons – actually, having grown up with no television at all — they found me quaintly ignorant. Even waking up next to a lover on a weekend morning could bring annoying reminders.

"Sorry, but who are Boris and Natasha?" from me.

From him, "You've never watched them? And you haven't heard of Robin Williams? Mork from Ork?"

My transition guide was a WASP from Westchester, Libby Cooper Watson. Button-nosed, brown-eyed, and bubbly, she was as comfortable a native as you could ever meet. We were classmates and became roommates, and confidantes. For a while she even persuaded me — each very briefly — to go to church with her, try smoking cigarettes, and go out with her cousin Douglas. In return I got her to try Marmite on her toast — briefly — and rooibos tea, soon an addiction. She became very dear, almost like a sister.

With my parents' blessing, I stayed on in America after the degree. For a while I taught in Boston at a Quaker school so wholesome I was almost persuaded to ditch Judaism and convert. And then Libby, who'd moved back to New York to rejoin her boy-next-door fiancé, talked me into applying for a job at her alma mater, a private school on the Upper West Side of Manhattan.

In 1979, not long after Libby got married, I met and married Charles Smith.

In this reminiscent mood, for a few minutes I revel in the pleasure of that promising beginning. He and I were a classic pair of Manhattan professionals, what the media were about to begin calling "DINKs," double-income-no-kids. We were educators and culture hounds, each with expertise we planned to parlay into books and lectures. Libby proudly declared me the most successful woman she knew.

Come to think of it, I'm overdue with the package of tea I send Libby on her birthday each year. I must remember to stock up. She has been calling every few days, worrying about me in my bereaved state, and I should reassure her. She has enough on her plate, dealing with adolescent grandchildren, without picturing me in decline. When I told her about my fall off the ladder, she offered to climb on a plane and come nurse me. I insisted I was coping just fine, though it would have been wonderful to see her.

Back to the L.A. restaurant. I unroll that strip of memory as I move about my little garden, raking leaves and straightening up. There isn't much to do, thanks to Jacob, but I'm happy to be outside after two days of chilly rain. It's been almost as cold here in Kalk Bay as it was in the New York I escaped to attend that Los Angeles conference, welcoming the California sunshine like manna for my South African soul.

With my face shielded by a big blue hat, I flexed my back, feeling the warmth penetrate the loose cape of my hair. It was making me drowsy, so I closed my folder, removed the hat, and looked about for a waiter.

"Sally? Copper Girl?" The voice was deep and hushed, disbelieving. I glanced over my shoulder, not quite sure I'd heard my name and saw a man wearing a broad-brimmed brown fedora. He was bow-legged and lean with a leather bag slung over one shoulder, and his hand was reaching out to my hair. "What are you doing here?"

"Felix?!"

The puppet master of our lives could not have timed the L.A. encounter at a stranger moment.

Charles was back in New York. Given what he'd confessed the day before in a phone call I cut short, I didn't care where he was, the son-of-a-bitch. I had my lecture to give that evening and a seminar the next morning on trends in music and dance education, and I'd been holding myself together, blocking out the pain and confusion, and all thought of what would happen next between him and me. Doing my Bunnington best to stay in control.

On that restaurant patio, all the misery vanished. I rose out of my chair and Felix and I slammed together like magnets. His hat and mine went flying. I was afraid to let go, in case this was a chimera and no one would be standing there. He held on just as tight, his lips on my hair and my neck and my mouth. I stiffened for a moment at the strangeness of this intimacy with someone who wasn't Charles, but the hunger and sheer delight swept away that barrier.

A waiter with a big tray "ahem"-ed and asked if he could get by. We disengaged, pulled back to let him pass, and turned back to stare at each other incredulously. Eventually we sat down, our hands clasped across the tiled surface of the table.

Aside from the shorter, darker hair, he looked the same. The mouth was curling with as much mischief as ever, his eyes still topaz and glittering. It dawned on me that in that bright light he would see how I had aged, with the premature white strands at my left temple. But he was just beaming.

"Look at you, lovelier than ever, my sweet girl."

Jesus, Sally Paddington, what are you doing here?"

"Well, it's Sally Paddington-Smith now, and not yours or anyone else's." I grinned at him, seeing his laughter welling up. He looked down at my hand and touched my wedding band.

He had one on too.

"Not my Sal or anyone else's? Where's this Mr. Smith, or is he also Paddington-Smith?"

"Just Smith, and as far as I'm concerned, he could be in Timbuktu. What about you?" And I touched his ring too. I wanted to run my fingers over his hand, to feel the weathered brown skin, so I did. He laid his other hand over mine, and I froze, not sure of the signal. Was he keeping my hand there, or preventing further intimacy?

"Where's your wife?" I asked.

"At home, in San Diego, with our daughter." Felix glanced into the distance. "Too busy to come on this trip. I did invite them. We could have taken Joanie to Disneyland."

He had a child. Deep inhale, absorbing that. A daughter.

"She's three and a bit." He dipped into his shoulder bag and brought out some photos. She looked just like him, a kitten version of the tiger man, with wild, white-blond ringlets and an ear-to-ear grin.

"How about you?" he asked.

"No. None yet." The racket of conversation and clinking of dishes and cutlery faded into the background as we absorbed the information and questions formed, unvoiced. Why had we lost each other? What was this now? Our hands were entwined, thumbs slowly rubbing, palms pressing together.

Then, talk bubbled up again and flowed as it always had,

from one topic to another. I told him about my job at Sutton Hill College. Mention of the Latina boss of our music department reminded me of Maria, the girl he'd been so devoted to. I asked about her and he said, "Not too good. She hasn't been well." I wanted to ask more, and about his parents, but I didn't dare go there. This harmony was too precious.

"I have two hours," he said at last. "Then I need to head over to UCLA. I'm giving a presentation this evening on muscle regeneration."

"I have two hours too," I said, astonished. "Then I have to be at UCLA, also to give a talk – on the therapeutic benefits of dance. Tomorrow I'm on a panel on intercultural influences, and then there's a workshop with a bunch of teachers from the L.A. schools."

"The International Interdisciplinary Conference?" he asked. We grinned slowly at each other, shaking our heads in wonder at the zany craziness of the coincidence. For all our miles-apart disciplines and utterly different brains, here we were participating in different parts of the same event, this huge conference on health and culture. I was so proud of Felix – and myself – and how far we'd come.

Without saying anything more, he laid down enough money to cover his check and mine, took my hand, and drew me out into the street. I followed, grabbing my own shoulder bag – a slick briefcase style, gifted to me by Charles on my last birthday – and then led the way two blocks up the palm-lined boulevard to my hotel.

That day might have been no more than a wonderful, fleeting encounter – a cameo in our lives. Had Felix's wife

Deidre sounded more devoted and his life with her happier, my conscience might have cooled my ardor. But he made it clear that were it not for Joanie, they would have split up. And of course, there was my cheating Charles. Right then, I didn't give a damn about him. Without explaining anything, I think I made that clear to Felix.

He and I sat together on the bed, slowly shedding garments, touching, talking, traipsing through shared memories. We talked about my parents and old friends from Rhodes. I told him about Winston, "your protégé," Felix had called him — and the letters I'd had from him describing painful stop-start progress.

He seemed to welcome my questions about his own life. I don't think he'd summed up his whole situation to anyone else in a while. He described Deidre as a livewire, a dynamic business woman who fascinated him when they met at a party, and their current relationship as "a state of suspended hostilities."

"She's smart," he said. "She took over marketing this muscle-therapy device I developed — the kind of thing your Winston might benefit from. I was grateful. I don't think I'd ever have gotten it out there without her. We were working together a lot, and she ended up moving in with me. She pushed for marriage. I resisted — you know me, I don't trust that legalistic stuff — but I gave in."

And then Joanie came along. Talking about her, Felix melted into a puddle of pride and delight. It made me so happy, and so jealous of her mother.

They sold the rights to his device and Deidre branched off

into other ventures, climbing her way up the entrepreneurial and social ladders. Who knows, she might have a different version of how things went wrong, but as he described it, she'd become more and more impatient with his absorption in his work and with his lack of interest in the prestige she craved. "Now she does her thing; I do mine," he said.

He turned to me, dismissing that topic, and his smile deepened as we sank to the horizontal. Felix's body was different, not quite as wiry, but still muscled. I expect he thought the same of mine. But our coordination was the same — perhaps even better. No condoms, but more control. My skin felt electric, as if a charge had been accumulating without a chance to release. Now the stroke of those hands, so tender and so appreciative, was brushing sparks up and along, all over. He took his time and I let him, interrupting him with questions and then interrupting his answers with more kissing. We made love, showered, talked, and made love again, until we were both drained.

As I dressed, regret began to seep in. We had gone way beyond the two-hour limits we'd both set, and a tepid yellow light washed across the room, casting shadows over the grandiose landscape prints on the wall. Anxiety loomed about my talk that evening. And the unease brought back thoughts of Charles. He had helped me prepare my talk, sharing tips on how to engage and hold an audience, and insisting I rehearse. He had been enthusiastic about my coming to L.A., though probably for reasons of his own.

But here I was, simmering with disdain for him and the little tart who'd gone to bed with him, and I was doing the same thing with another woman's mate. A sliver of anger poked through the haze – at Charles, but even more at myself.

Felix noticed my withdrawal. He asked what was wrong, and I started to answer. "This was bad. We shouldn't have…"

"Jesus, Sally!" He zipped up his pants and tugged his belt buckle closed. "I can't believe you're still second-guessing every damn move. That's why it didn't work between us back then. This was wonderful, and who the hell did we hurt?"

I thought he was right, and it felt depressingly familiar. Here I was, a successful professional, a New Yorker, a woman with life experience, and I was pushing him away just as I did all those years ago.

I said, "I am glad we did this." I grabbed the lapels of his jacket, drawing him closer. We started kissing, and he suggested we meet up after our talks, that he come back to my room and we spend the night together. I agreed, relieved. Together in the taxi to the conference center, we held hands in happy silence.

Not surprisingly, after the afternoon we'd had and our evening performances, by the time we'd had a drink and compared notes on our respective presentations, we were both exhausted. We fell asleep snuggled up tight, contented, without making love. During the night, I turned over in the middle of a dream – something with wild waves and sea spray – and was woken by the feeling of this beloved, familiar-unfamiliar body next to me. For a moment I thought it was a continuation of my dream, but he was awake and grinning at my shock. He began kissing my eyes and my nose and my shoulders. We drifted back to sleep around five.

The phone woke us an hour later. It was Charles, his voice all deep and deliberately intimate. "I'm about to leave for work," he said. "But I wanted to check in with you, and to tell you I love you, and wish you good luck for your talk this morning."

Aside from the fact that my big talk had been the night before and he'd ignored the time difference and woken me, it was a sweet gesture. I stammered, "Thanks, Charles. How are you doing?" He started to apologize again, begging me not to be angry, but I interrupted him. "Look, I have to go. We'll talk when I get home."

Felix had gone to the bathroom. He came back with a towel wrapped around his hips, just as in the old days, water glistening on the line of hair rising toward his navel. He looked down at me, his eyebrows raised in question, and gave a nod of acknowledgment.

We exchanged addresses and talked about staying in touch, and he left. The heavy hotel door with its "Do Not Disturb" card thudded shut behind him and I flopped down on the mess of bed clothes. I was in turmoil, missing him already, even as guilt surged over me. *This is bullshit*, I told myself. *You should be better than this. Never again.*

~ 10 ~

Backpack

Thinking of the conference in L.A. and that morning at the restaurant, I frown as I don the old linen hat. I'm heading outside to scrub the peeling varnish off the wooden window frames, in preparation for staining and re-varnishing. The metal hinges need to be de-rusted, and I should probably re-caulk the panes of glass. Or I could leave it all as is for the next owner.

Though clouds are spilling in over the mountain, the light is still sharp, and these days I really do have to be careful about my skin, hence the hat. It's one of the few things I brought with me from the States. You can roll it up and unroll it and the shape is none the worse. It was sky blue; now it's almost white, except where the ribbon used to sit around the crown. I loved it for its practicality, unlike Felix, who loved hats for their swagger.

"Look at me," he would crow, plonking a new one over his gray hair as we prowled the Saturday craft market down by the harbor. He'd strut about as if trying on a fabulous foreign persona. From the hat seller we'd be lured to the breakfast tent by the smell of bacon intertwined with the aroma of coffee and toasted muffins.

Just for fun, for once with no chore in mind, I clamber up the shaky steps to the attic. There's Felix's hat collection – caps and homburgs and sombreros. They come from Mexico and Italy and Australia, hanging on hooks that run the length of the wall. Goodness knows how he accumulated so much, and he was still eager to gather more.

My favorite is still that fedora he had on in L.A. He got it before *Indiana Jones* made the image so famous and still wore it these last years – with even more flare, his pony tail trailing below it. I run my fingers along the swashbuckling, age-mottled brim before placing it back on its hook.

I squeeze my sun hat in between Felix's chapeaux, just for the pleasure of the proximity. I feel again the bliss of that long-ago L.A. afternoon – and the horrible emptiness afterwards. There is a musty smell emanating from the wall, possibly mold from that darn leak. My plastering hasn't worked. You can see moisture seeping through again. The hats should all be removed – and probably discarded.

My mother would have understood this collection. Imma adored hats, and though she knew my generation wasn't into them, she insisted on buying them for me. I had a sequined beret and a Gigi-style half-moon hat. The sun hat was my purchase, and she would have thought it awfully boring — something to hide under rather than flaunt.

Hats were part of her triumph as a survivor. I can still see her in her favorite, a lime-green straw saucer with purple silk flowers under the brim. She wore it at an angle, looking very Ingrid Bergmanesque. "As long as I don't look like Queen Elizabeth," she said. "That poor woman can never wear anything that shades her face. Did you know that?"

My mother would have adored New York. I did too, for all its loudness and bombast.

My first home in the city was a studio on Hudson Street in the West Village. "You the same sex all the way up?" a construction worker called to me one morning. He probably guessed I was the real deal because the transsexuals in the neighborhood were way more glamorous. I might not have been as adaptable as Felix, but I had my different selves. In the Big Apple I could be prim Bunnington, the music teacher, or svelte Sally, the red-haired torch singer doing an occasional night club gig, or a would-be Mother Teresa, working with underprivileged kids at a YMCA in the Bronx. I could be anyone there.

But you could also be lonely in the midst of the crowds. Libby got engaged and more or less vanished. My students were fine, and my new friends were fun, but none of them needed me. In New York, who would really care if I disappeared? For a while I got depressed. Not acute misery like after the break-up with Felix, just a grayness that wouldn't lift.

In desperation, following advice in a magazine, I signed on to help at a shelter for battered women one night a week. They were so clearly worse off than me. On Saturdays I read to a group of elderly men with vision problems. All they wanted was sports stories. It was boring, but they flirted with me, always extracting the promise that I'd come back the next weekend. I came home with gifts of hard candy and resolutions to find some other way to fill my time.

That's when Charles entered my life.

On Christmas Day I helped out at a soup kitchen. Charles was next to me in the line of volunteers, scooping roast turkey and stuffing onto paper plates. He smiled down at me with his dark, gentle eyes and I beamed back up at him. Even with an apron, he looked elegantly well-dressed.

"Would you fancy a hot chocolate?" I asked as we cleared away the big emptied pots.

"I would kill for one," he said, "but where? I don't think Chinese restaurants serve it and almost everything else is closed." He had a deep, resonant voice and his words came out rounded and purposeful.

"*Chez moi.* I'm two blocks away. And I even have those little marshmallows to put on top."

That was forward, and possibly risky. I'd never made the first move with any guy before, let alone invited a stranger into my home. But Charles was soothing. This is a ridiculous reason, but I'd noticed he had a heavy limp, and there was something childlike about his face — a fresh, eager quality that ran counter to his deep voice and made me feel motherly.

He stayed over that first night, not in my bed , but on the

pull-out sofa. We'd been adding booze to our chocolate — a liqueur someone had given me — and it was snowing, and he was tired. And I wasn't inclined to kick him out.

In the morning, he had padded into my bedroom with that uneven lub-dub footfall, with his black hair all mussed up, looking like a rumpled puppy. I pushed back the blankets and invited him in. He wasn't very skillful, but I was so happy to embrace and be embraced, it was fine by me.

"You're my Christmas present," I told him.

"Well, Hanukkah actually. I'm Jewish," he said.

Who'd have guessed? My parents would almost have approved.

We went out for brunch later. You know those couples you see on weekend mornings, damp-haired and so into each other, you just know what they've been doing? That was us, and it felt good.

Charles told me all about how he had polio as a child. His skeletal issues were the kind Felix had been doing research on when we last met in South Africa. At my request, back then he'd sent me a couple of his research papers and some articles about other work in his field.

"For an arts person, you're very knowledgeable," my new lover said, and talked at length about the challenges he faced. I mentioned that I'd learned stuff about muscle function from an old boyfriend. He drew back for a moment at that, but then went right on talking, to my relief. I didn't want him to think I'd been with a lot of men.

One leg was shorter than the other and the imbalance, he said, caused hip and spine problems. "It's a drag, but I don't let it get me down," he stated. I found his courage touching, and I wanted to give him my arm to lean on for as long as he needed it.

He was fascinated by my dancing and eager to see me perform. That interest in dancing reminded me of Felix, but with Charles there was something else — an almost vicarious delight, as if I moved for him. He loved showing me off to his friends. In the months that followed, he came to every recital I was involved with, either as a performer or a teacher, and often invited other people to come too.

That was fine by me. He was an adjunct professor of philosophy at City University of New York, and he was just as eager for me to attend any public lectures he gave. He reveled in the sharing, or maybe the showing-off. I took it as sharing.

Perhaps most winning of all, he held the view that monogamous commitment was the mark of an evolved human being. He gave me books on philosophy and left little slips of paper to mark the passages confirming that view.

At his urging, two months after the soup kitchen encounter, I blithely gave up my studio apartment and moved into his much larger place, a walk-up on East 78th Street. The rent was twice as high, but split in two it wasn't much added hardship. It pleased me that it lightened the load for him. Not that he needed any financial help. His father was a surgeon and the family was rich, even if we weren't. I was happy and in love or, if not in love, enamored with our life and optimistic about the future.

We got married seven months later. The wedding was in Connecticut, a sunset ceremony at his parents' home, set on the shores of a lake. Imma wasn't well at the time, so she and Pops couldn't be there, but standing under the *chuppah*, with the tall elm trees silhouetted black against gold-tinged clouds and the faces around us smiling benignly, I thought to them, "*You can stop worrying about me now.*"

❧

How do you wrap up seven decades of life? The more I shed of Felix's possessions, the more I find. My back muscles protest each box and case and bag I carry out to the garbage bin or lug to the charity store. And then his presence manifests in a new direction. It's like he's saying, "Can't get rid of me that easily," and I welcome it. If it weren't for having to make the house marketable, I'd hold on to every last scrap!

The highlight of the day: I found another stash of cash in the drawer of the table I've uncovered up in the attic. It was under clothes and albums, a truly strange piece Felix made, goodness knows when, from pieces of driftwood. It's sturdy though and oddly pleasing. The drawer is shallow, fitted with partitions, perfect for pens and paper clips – and money. This time it comes with a note in his usual scrawl: "In case of emergency, splurge!"

How did he know I would find it? Did he sense he was going to leave me? Did he worry about my future? I sit for a long while at the table, breathing in the pine smell that emanates from the drawer. If he was feeling symptoms – headaches? – why didn't he mention them to me? That's not really a mystery: I would have tried even harder to make him slow down, and he had no interest in doing that. Two waves clash inside me, of anger and gratitude.

One task has been completed: I've cleared the junk out of the spare room, so when Joanie comes I can make her comfortable. I wish Trevor was coming also. It's two years since his last visit, and Felix's youngest has gone through all kinds of changes since then, giving up on an engineering degree and switching instead to architecture, like his brother-in-law. He's impulsive – always has been – full of enthusiasms that light him up, and sometimes lead him astray. I can't bear the thought that he might drift out of my life. I'd make sleeping space for him in the living room if he'd come, but I know he's somewhat broke and very busy.

The "spare room," next to our bedroom, was to be my study when I moved in with Felix, a place I could withdraw to when needed. The need never arose. The work I had intended doing was forgotten. Instead the room became a repository for the stuff he couldn't put elsewhere or fit in the attic. The prime example is a chair made of driftwood and webbed rubber strips from old tires that Felix brought home from one of his jaunts. It was too hideous to put in the living room, but he insisted it was too comfortable to discard. There is also a brass bell that visiting kids love to clang and one of those green glass floats from a fishing net. I suspect Felix found both at the local flea market, though he liked to pass off the nautical stuff as flotsam left by the previous owners.

I want to test the chair before leaving it for my guest. I take diary "#2, 1964, Spain" from the box under my bed, with the intention of settling in that chair and reading for a while before taking a walk. As usual, hauling out the journal box, I push aside the other box stowed away beside it, making yet another mental note that I must check its contents and, if possible, discard them.

Ensconced in the webbing chair, I doze off — proof, I suppose, that Felix was right; it is comfortable. The distant train siren rouses me and I start reading again. He's in Italy.

> *"These people really know how to use their hands. The leather work in Florence is the best I've ever seen. Took my boots to an old guy around the corner from the hotel and watched as he mended them like new. He didn't watch what he was doing, just chatted away in broken English as his fingers flew. Charged so little I felt obliged to buy something. Got a great backpack for Maria. It would work well for her. Haven't decided — send it to her or keep it till our paths cross again? Might just keep it."*

I don't know what he means about it working for her, but ah, the backpack. I remember it well. I stop reading, search a while, and sure enough, there it is, deep in a box with other relics, stiff now and unusable, but still dear in its familiarity. He had it slung over his shoulder the first day we met, and for a moment, that morning in Los Angeles, I thought he was carrying the same one. But that was new, he said, purchased by his wife in protest against the shabbiness of this beloved Italian purchase. She tried to throw it out, but Felix resisted. As willingly as he traveled, more and more he weighed himself down with an accumulation of stuff. It's as if he craved ballast to counteract his lack of a home base.

Funny, remembering how he arrived at Rhodes with little more than that backpack. I took it to be a rebellion against materialism, and was impressed. Turns out he had plenty of stuff, stored at John Latimer's. I, on the other hand, actually had — and have — very little. I've shed things all along the way, perhaps the way I shed relationships, and homes.

That gives me pause. I've had us classified so neatly all these years, him as the wanderer, me as Ms. Stability — but in some ways the truth is the other way around. With this move five years ago I basically abandoned everything in my Brooklyn abode. I asked my friend Sherrie to give it away and only ship out to Kalk Bay the essentials I listed for her.

Imma and Pops arrived in South Africa with almost nothing. Then they gathered as much as they could, filling our home with the trappings of permanence. I wanted none of it, till now. I feel so empty, the South-Easter could blow me away.

When I returned to New York from the L.A. trip, Charles was contrite. There were flowers all over the apartment, sickly sweet bunches of lilies, and he insisted that we sit down and talk the moment I walked in. I was tired and cold, not in the mood for a heart-to-heart, but he wouldn't wait.

"Please believe me, Sally, it was really just a meaningless dalliance," he said, clasping my hands in his. "It didn't go on long. I knew I made a mistake almost the minute it began. I've told her it's over. That's why I called you. I don't want there to be any secrets between us."

On the phone he'd made out it was a one-night stand. Evidently not, and angry sarcasm frothed up. I was about to start peppering him with questions and further accusations, but I froze. He recoiled as if bracing for an attack, his head ducked into his shoulders, but I went silent. All the sarcastic, cutting accusations that had been simmering for days cooled, subsided, disappeared. How could I possibly attack him for committing infidelity? I just wanted to go to sleep.

Anyway, I could see how things had gone wrong. Charles was teaching at New York University by then, and his subject matter — or the way he taught it, as if his heart lay in every line — seemed to make his students very emotional. For some, that impact was augmented by his lopsided gait. They'd offer to carry his books and open doors for him. One of the girls, this Tracy Someone, had been coming by his office to help out a bit too often. It was true he and I had been ridiculously busy, running on separate tracks and seldom together. And then I went away for that week, according to him just when he was battling a bout of depression.

"You didn't notice I'd been really down," he whined. We hadn't turned on the lights in the apartment and his face was in shadow. "The weather was lousy. *The Journal of Philosophy* turned down my article. My raise didn't come through. Tracy was the one bright spark in my week."

I pulled my hands away and switched on a lamp. It was one of a pair of Tiffany lamps we'd received as a wedding gift from his grandmother. Turning them on always made me happy, but not that night. I snarled at him, "That's a pathetic excuse, and so stupid. Apart from anything else, you could have lost your job." He nodded in agreement, his shoulders sagging.

Clearly, he expected more rage from me. Instead he got this cold terseness. It didn't occur to him that I might have secrets of my own. I considered saying, "I've got a confession too." If he was being honest, shouldn't I be? But I just couldn't bring myself to tell him about Felix. Instead, I busied myself making supper, keeping my flushed face turned away from him.

This might be rationalizing in retrospect, but I don't think I'd have slept with Felix if I hadn't been so hurt and angry at Charles. But the fact is I had cheated too, so how could I go hurling fireballs at him? And what good would it do to hurt Charles the way he'd hurt me?

~ 11 ~

A Chubby Bear

In the days that followed, Charles was on his best behavior, sad eyes following me like a basset hound's, volunteering to do the shopping and the laundry, waiting for the eruption. In our years together he'd never seen me really enraged, but he was obviously on the alert, tense. Every time he sat down with me, his left shoe, the one with the built-up sole, would be tapping a staccato. I could see his cheek muscles clenching. But he got no heat from me.

The bliss of that afternoon with Felix still simmered inside me. I could feel the rumpled pillow under my cheek, smell his skin as he hovered above me, smiling into my smile, his breath coming faster… Even with my remorse about his wife, and my sheepishness that my marriage appeared to be intact, a shiver of delight arose whenever my thoughts drifted back to him.

Charles, on the other hand, was full of good resolutions. Step One in his plan was that we get more serious about having a child. I can still hear him, with his talk about my cycles and optimizing our timing, and even about vaginal mucous. But true to style, there was more theory than practice. The mood never seemed right.

We'd wanted a baby all along, not in an urgent, high-priority way, but as a taken-for-granted next chapter in married life. His siblings had kids; we'd have them too. When it didn't happen, we shrugged and assumed at some point it would. We strolled on weekend afternoons from our apartment to the playground in Central Park and watched the kids cavorting and playing, their parents hovering protectively. We smiled as the grown-ups wiped snotty noses and gritty hands. That was going to be us one of these days.

But month after month had passed. When I voiced concern, Charles cut short any question regarding him. He'd been married before, very briefly and unhappily to some brilliant but bitchy girl, and back then, he said, he'd had his sperm count checked. He assured me it wasn't a problem. I took him at his word. The urologist he consulted was a friend of his father's and evidently just told him to keep trying, that everything would come right.

I got the same kind of reassurance. The gynecologist his father suggested I see, in her cramped and probably very expensive offices on Park Avenue, didn't find anything obviously wrong. She just suggested Charles and I pay more attention to our timing, and frequency. "Frequency can cure a lot," she said.

This was easier said than done. Even before the infidelity, our union wasn't exactly high octane. Sad, in a way, given how enthusiastically we began. Charles seemed to assume I was repressed, that it was part of the ladylike poise he so respected in me. I knew better – but wasn't about to describe my sexual history. On the other hand, I thought our lack of action was due to his physical problems, but there was no way I'd voice that to my debonair husband. We'd become more companionable than lusty.

With the doctor's advice in mind and hoping to stir some passion, one chilly weekend in spring I suggested we borrow his parents' beach bungalow in the Hamptons. We went often enough over each summer. Those stays were fun – crowded and noisy and full of laughter. But I'd always thought it would be wonderful to be there alone when it was peaceful. Charles was surprised, but he agreed quite readily. We rented a car, stocked up on food on the way, and brought wine and a fine bottle of cognac someone had given us. "We're not driving anywhere. We can get plastered if we want," I said.

The first night, we were both tired from the drive, and opted to go to sleep early. The next morning, I awoke thinking it might be an opportune time, but he was fast asleep and snoring heavily. I slithered out of bed, bundled up with a hat and scarf, and went for a hike along the beach. Walking on soft sand wasn't easy for Charles, so I welcomed the chance to do it alone. On the way back I detoured to the village bakery, intending to wake him with fresh bagels and breakfast in bed.

But when I got in, he was already up and making us pancakes. The bagels never got eaten. I broke them in pieces and tossed them to the gulls.

That evening, we barbecued, brought out the cognac, put on some Antonio Carlos Jobim, and snuggled by the fire. This, I thought, could surely lead to more. I began stroking his chest and opening buttons. The phone rang, and with a little smile of apology, he disentangled himself and went to answer. It was one of his colleagues with an urgent curriculum question, and they talked for an hour. I went to bed. No one's fault – other than his for giving the guy the Hamptons phone number – and I can't say I really cared.

Despite our lack of activity, here I was, faced with the fact that my very regular period hadn't arrived. At first, I thought it was because of stress and an unusually exhausting schedule, and I let the weeks go by. It was May, the time for new beginnings. The scrawny little azalea bush in the pot on our balcony began to produce tight green buds. Then I missed a second period.

When last had Charles and I made love? Not hard to remember: A few days before that trip to L.A. I suspected, looking back, that it was because he was turned on by that student of his and was lusting after her. So he got his rocks off with me, and still went after her.

Dressing in the morning was becoming more difficult. The "teaching" end of my closet, the neat tailored skirts and dresses, all felt too tight. For the first time in my life my body felt clumsy. As if that wasn't bad enough, I found myself detouring to pick up a McDonald's burger on my way to school because I was hungry half an hour after breakfast. Any last doubt fizzled out one morning when I gave myself a spritz of the Chanel I'd been using for years, and it turned my stomach. Even without a test, I knew for certain.

My friends would have been delighted — but I had cause not to tell them, just as I had cause not to tell Charles. My mind kept sliding back to what had seemed like such skillful timing on Felix's part, not too soon but just in time. Maybe not so skillful.

Who could I confide in? Libby was out of the question. She revered Charles and, with two kids of her own already, had been praying that we'd be "blessed" too. I couldn't imagine telling my mother the whole story, though I longed to be around her, to bask in her love. The distance hurt worse than ever.

Instead, drawing on every drop of Bunnington poise, I went about my days maintaining a rigid barrier between inner and outer realities. The inner landscape was sub-divided too, between over-the-moon excitement at the thought of a little life starting inside me, and the horror of not knowing who its father might be.

Finally, I did confide in a friend, my old Rhodes pal Angie, because I knew she'd remember Felix and wouldn't mince her words. She was still in Grahamstown. I called her from my office at work, with the door locked, and reached her at home in the evening. With the faint roar of traffic punctuated by sirens and car horns outside my window, I pictured her with the chilly quiet of autumn outside hers and a fire crackling in the deep fireplace of her old Cape cottage. "This is a long-distance call. Go play somewhere else," I heard her say, and then she turned to me, her attention as intense as ever.

She barked, "Abort! You have absolutely no other choice." I hunched over the receiver to muffle her voice, lest anyone passing by outside hear her. "And do it very soon, before it gets harder to do, before Charles and everyone else can see that you are expecting."

The idea cracked my heart. I started to argue, but she was adamant. "How can you go ahead with this, never knowing if this kid is his or that idiot Felix's? You can't live with a doubt the rest of your life. The child could turn out to be blond, like his daughter – and that would look pretty weird with your family, and from what you've said, with Charles's tribe."

She broke off to light up a cigarette and then launched right back in. "You know Felix isn't about to leave his wife because of that kid he already has with her. Face it, Sal, this was an accident, a stupid mistake. But now you know you can get pregnant, and the next time it will be Charles's brat, no complications, no problem."

Angie, the cynic, had made a very sensible marriage herself. She'd settled down with her math tutor, who'd become a math professor. She had two kids and a granny flat for her mother, "who's still drinking," she told me. "But she serves her purpose – reminding me every day not to touch the stuff." Her baby logic seemed irrefutable, but my brain kept recoiling from her points.

I took a day off and made an appointment at a clinic downtown in Tribeca, miles away from our Upper East Side apartment. I was stiff with apprehension. I expected they'd do a test and spell out my options. If I said yes to it, would they be willing to do the procedure right then or make me wait and come back another day?

The city streets were oddly empty, as if everyone was avoiding me. No one asked for money. No one bumped into me or met my eyes. The waiting room at the clinic was starkly businesslike, with the requisite plastic plant and public service posters in English and Spanish. The other women looked as miserable as I felt. Only those with companions were chatting. The rest of us huddled in our silent cocoons. The longer I sat there, the colder I got, the tighter my muscles clenched, and the more wrong everything felt.

How could I, the child of survivors, the only grandchild from a family that should have had a dozen, snuff out this light? If I found the courage to tell my mother the truth, once she got over being horrified about my transgression, I knew what she would say: "A life is a life. We will love this child no matter what." My father? He would be disappointed in me — but loving too. Charles's family? I'd have to hope they never found out the truth.

Before they could call me in, with my neck muscles knotted, I gathered my bag and jacket and book, and slipped out, with just a muttered "Please cross Paddington-Smith off the list" to the receptionist.

On the subway home, rocking in sync with the gray army of other New Yorkers, staring at the row of black shoes and grubby sneakers, suddenly everyone seemed to be staring at me. I was quite sure all of them could see the cloud of confusion enveloping me. The train crept through Grand Central, and then 51st Street, and then 59th. At 79th, I couldn't wait to escape back up to street level. The cool wind on my face soothed my nausea, but I still didn't know what to do with my free day. Instead of going home, I turned and went into the cinema two blocks from the apartment.

They were showing *The Big Chill*. In the gloom, I could make out about twelve other people, the day-time escapees. I got nauseous again as the movie progressed, either from the miasma of buttery popcorn or the fact that one of the characters urges her husband to have sex with their single friend who is desperate to have a child. My stomach was in knots.

I'm having a baby. Hopefully a healthy one. Surely that's all that counts, I told myself.

The walk home was interminable. I clambered up the three flights of stairs with my belly cramping tighter with each step, made it through the door and collapsed on the toilet. It felt as if everything from my heart down came gushing out. Finally, weepy but feeling better, I reached around to wipe, and saw on the wad of paper a splash of crimson and a dark red, lumpy smear of…?

Dilemma ended.

At that point, I told Charles. I had to. Not the Felix part, just that I'd conceived, and miscarried. The weeping kept erupting again. We were sitting at the dining room table that night, with a collection of half-emptied Chinese takeout containers in front of us. He was eating. I couldn't force down more than a few mouthfuls.

He kept saying, "Why didn't you tell me?" as if his knowing would somehow have saved the baby.

"I'm sorry. I'm so sorry." I put my head down on my arms and sobbed, for the baby, and him, and me. I said, "I was scared to believe it was true, after all this time. Scared if I said anything, that would jinx it. And I was still angry with you. I'm sorry, Charles."

He came around to my side of the table and hugged me tight, murmuring, "It's all right, Sally. It's all right. I understand."

He forgave me for not telling him. And I forgave him for the Tracy business. And thanked Fate that he didn't know what else there was to forgive me for. As wobbly as I felt, my image was preserved. I was his lady wife, an *eshet chayil*, as they say in Hebrew, a woman of valor.

There were doctors' visits, weeks of tearfulness, and uncharacteristic mood swings. Charles's mother Ethel, whom he had told, took me to tea at the Plaza, thinking it would cheer me up. It should have. The place was so grand, the little cakes and pastries so perfect, and the clientele as buffed as the marble columns, but it made me feel even more misshapen. Tears dripped down my nose and into my porcelain cup.

Ethel put her arms around me and said, "My poor, poor Sally, you're suffering from postpartum depression." That seemed far-fetched; I hadn't been more than ten weeks pregnant. "Tell your body that," she said. I accepted it. Having spent so many years alongside Dad-in-law Ben, she spoke with almost as much medical authority as he did. "Your hormones, your uterus, everything was in welcome mode, ready to nurture this growth."

Growth? I wanted to yell at her. It was more than a growth;

it was my child, her grandchild — her fourth, but still. My reaction bore out what she was saying. For all the ambivalence, my brain had been moving into welcoming mode as well. The baby was a girl, I'm sure. Leila, I don't know why, but definitely Leila. Her eyes would have been brown — or topaz. And I had betrayed her, poisoned her with my ambivalence.

Charles was sweet and patient, almost buoyed up. He commented, as Angie had, on how it opened up hope, now that we knew I could conceive. For a while he came home earlier and pampered me, only mentioning once that he had noticed I was getting a little plumper.

Around then the "Paddington Bear" label began, in the aftermath of the pregnancy. I kept going to yoga, but I wasn't dancing at all except to demonstrate steps for my students. Various people found pleasure in noting how "well" I looked with fuller cheeks. One of my colleagues even bought me a little bear, with a blue coat and red hat, to prove she saw the nickname as a measure of affection. Maybe it was true. In various ways, I found myself softer, more open to accepting human fallibility.

I propped the little bear on my desk and communed with him when I couldn't with anyone else. "You're a lost soul from deepest, darkest Peru," I reminded him. "And I'm a lost soul from deepest, darkest Africa."

When I took to wearing my blue sun hat, pulled down over my red hair, Charles came home one day with a red coat for me, presented with a big, proud smile, "to complete your outfit." It was sweet of him, and should have lifted my spirits, but I found it very hard to wear anything hat eye-catching. This

Paddington didn't want to be seen.

Through all that, even as I tried so hard to put my heart back into my marriage, I yearned to speak to Felix. The school library had a stack of phone books from cities around the country. I went so far as to look for his number in a San Diego directory. It was there. I could have called. But the risk of getting his wife on the line was too great. And what would I have said anyway? "By the way, I might have just miscarried your baby"?

In the late afternoon, as a rosiness streaks the sky, I hear a rap at the front door and then a voice from inside. Edith, never one to hang back, has let herself in and is yelling up the stairs, "Paddington? Where the hell are you? The boys and I were walking by and decided to find out if you're still alive. Come walk with us."

I grab a jacket and head out with her and the pug brothers. Come to think of it, they look a bit like furry babies, toddling on all fours. They're a nuisance to walk with, weaving in and out of our feet, sniffing everything, peeing on everything. But it does me good to get out and move, inhale some salty air. We talk as we walk, about dogs and weather. My voice feels raspy. It's the first time I've used it in days.

~ 12 ~

Coffee Cups

Joanie arrives on a Sunday afternoon. That timing makes the long drive to the airport and back to Kalk Bay a little easier – but not much. What pressure is eased on the highway by the absence of commuters is made up for by the weekend sightseers cruising the coast road. I don't really care once I have her with me. We natter all the way, as I ease my Volvo through the congestion.

"How come you never had any children? You did want to, didn't you?" Joanie asks me, out of the blue. I had been wanting to ask her the same question – except not in the past tense – but wasn't sure it was an acceptable topic. She is not too old but why delay?

"Yes, I did," I say. I was two years older than her when I got pregnant. "But it didn't work out." I'd like to share the memory with her but don't want to risk opening up the awkwardness of that Charles-Felix confusion, or to make her afraid that already at her age miscarriage becomes more likely. The postscript that came after my loss is way too dark to get into on this joyful sunny afternoon.

"I'll tell you more about it another time," I say.

There's a ritual I know she will enjoy. I pull off the main road, wind down to the Muizenberg beach front, and park. With no need for discussion, we two sashay across to the Brown Cow Dairy Store, and I order two cones, peppermint chocolate chip for her, classic vanilla for me, and coffee, because I'm craving some. We sit on the high, round stools facing the big picture window, and she smiles and licks, and smiles, looking out at red and blue and yellow cabanas and the wetsuit-clad surfers carrying their gleaming boards. This is something she and I have done at some point every time she's come to visit. Today it delays for a little longer that inevitable moment when she'll walk into the house and encounter the awful gap.

She tells me about her latest round of conflict with her mother. "We're worse than ever," she says. "She's so self-centered and I have no patience with her these days." I've been her listener on this topic for years, though I do my best to stay tactful about Deidre. I tell her about Mergatroid's progress, and about my talk with the minister. She chortles when I confess to my irritation with him, and we toss around a few ideas of how we think that her father would have liked to be remembered.

"With dance," Joanie says. I'm astonished. Somehow, I don't think that's what Rev. What's-his-name had in mind. "You know how fascinated Dad was by the body's capabilities? He worked with so many injured dancers, and he told me I don't know how many times what a lovely dancer you were. You're still doing some choreography, aren't you? How about we put together a little performance?"

"Who could we get to dance?"

Joanie nibbles the edges of her cone, exposing another half inch of green ice cream. "I'll do it," she says, glancing up at me. She doesn't look as much like Felix as she did as a kid, not with make-up and long blond hair falling in lovely waves around her shoulders, but the expression is pure Felix, full of daring. "With you. I'll dance if you'll dance. And then if we can find one or two more, just something very simple."

My heart is hammering, either because of the sugar and caffeine, or something else, a rising glimmer of vitality I'm not quite ready to release.

Talking with Joanie is like having access to a live library. After all these weeks of solo searching, now I'm not just delving into old journals, or trying to piece together misty fragments of my own memories. Here is someone with actual recall of big stretches of Felix's life that I know only in broad outline.

"Why did your mom and dad break up?" The morning after her arrival, I set up the coffee machine for two cups. She reaches in front of me with a wry smile and ups that to three. Ah, a fellow addict. I didn't even think to ask her if she wanted some yesterday. I was remembering two years ago when she and

Eric came to visit before their wedding. It was health food all the way, no toxins, no additives. Felix got a little sarcastic with her, citing what digestive juices do to chemicals, etc., but in fact our diet (thanks to me) was pretty good anyway.

Does this mean she isn't thinking of babies yet? I sneak a look at her floaty cotton top, wondering if she's not a little bit more buxom than last time I saw her. Hard to tell, and none of my business. Maybe contentment has laid on a few extra pounds.

We settle ourselves at the kitchen table. Mergatroid crunches her way through a few last nuggets and manages, with some difficulty, to jump onto Joanie's lap. I'm vaguely hurt, but glad if it makes our guest feel even more welcome.

"Okay," she says, "this is how I saw it — but remember, I was only seven when they split up. Seemed to me Mom was zooming off in all directions, and Dad was doing his best to stay grounded for me. I know he used to travel a lot, and he was doing very little of that. While Mom did her business thing, he looked after me. And then Mom just announced she was moving to San Francisco, and taking me with her."

"Did your dad try to stop her?" How could she even know? But I'm puzzled. It wouldn't be Felix's style to hold onto someone against their will, but what about Joanie? He must have been enraged.

"He let her go," Joanie says, both hands around her cup. She looks back up at me, frowning in thought. "For a while, I was really hurt that he let me go and angry. I couldn't understand why he didn't fight harder. He tried to explain it all to me way later on, that he just couldn't see subjecting me to a push-and-pull battle, with all the court business and lawyers. You know how bad he was with that stuff anyway.

"He went off to Switzerland for a while to do some research there and somewhere else. That was horrible. He was gone for like six months."

Was that when he was with Maria? This damn man had no idea how to be alone for five minutes. I just nod and say nothing, to encourage her to keep talking. "But then he got a transfer back, and insisted on being based in San Francisco so he could be near me, and we spent a lot of time together."

Of course, he complicated his life all over again: He promptly got involved with one of his research assistants, a woman way younger than him, and along came Trevor.

I ask Joanie how she felt about that, very tentatively, but she bursts out laughing and I relax. With Felix around, I never felt I could probe this way, and it's like being set free in a park I've only seen through the fence. Everything about it is lush and fascinating, meshed in branches and blossoms and gnarled roots, the Rousseau painting that was Felix's life. She has lit up, evidently enjoying the subject too.

"Trevor was my doll! I thought Dad and Nellie'd had him specifically for my sake, to give me someone to look after and play with. I'd wanted a brother for so long, and now I had one, even if I could only see him on alternate weeks. They did it that way, you know; one week with Mom, one week with Dad and Nellie. I had double everything — but just one baby brother."

I tell her how much I wanted siblings too, and about the secret journal of my adventures with Betsy and Jeffrey.

Without thinking I say, "I was so cross with your dad for ignoring his sister and his brothers. I wanted to meet them and he wouldn't take me there."

Joanie puts down her coffee, her forehead furrowed. "I wouldn't say 'ignored,' but yeah, kept his distance. I know there was trouble of some kind. We did eventually go to Port Elizabeth on vacation, Dad and Trevor and me, to see my grandmother. And we met uncles and my aunt and their families." She looks quizzically at me, still surprised by my ignorance. "But that was only after Grandpa had died. I asked Dad why he waited so long. He said his father was a bigot, and he wouldn't have accepted Trevor. But Grandma was a sweetheart, and Dad was like a puppy around her, hugging and kissing her. 'Making up for lost time,' he said. He took lots of photos. They must be around here somewhere."

Then she added, "Of course, there was the other sister, who died. Remember? What was her name? That was such an awful story."

A sister who died? Shock radiates, touching on a circle of different issues. How could I not have known? Why didn't he tell me? Did I fail to read the signs that he was grieving over a loss?

I say, "I don't know if this is just my ailing old brain, but I can't recall her name — or what happened to her." That's totally dishonest and I feel bad, but I'm embarrassed by the blank. All I remember, very vaguely, is being confused about how many sisters he had — and being so burned when I did try to find out more, I gave up on the subject. Avoiding painful topics was the way of life in my family, the kinder way to be.

"Joanne," Joanie exclaims. "That was her name. I'm named after her."

Yet another lesson. So it wasn't John Latimer he was honoring, but this lost sister. Something is tickling my memory — those scratched-out comments in his journal, J-something, but I leave it alone again. Enough to rethink, enough to absorb.

The next area to tackle is the garage. There's a pungent smell of cat pee. I suspect Mergatroid's amour, a ragged-eared tabby who seems to have taken up residence but flees when I come near. There are so many boxes and suitcases and open containers, there's barely room for the Volvo.

Felix's latest motorbike, his last one, is still parked alongside the outer wall, covered in a tarpaulin to keep out the sea air. I haven't been near it since he died. A couple of guys have asked what I plan to do with it, and I've put them off, saying I haven't decided. But it shouldn't just sit like this, unused, growing rusty.

Riding the bike was the one thing he wouldn't share. Same as it was in Grahamstown, and apparently when he was traveling too. In one of his journals, the Europe one, I've read about a hair-raising journey on a borrowed bike through the winding mountain road between Lichtenstein and Germany. He was riding with some guy he'd met in Italy, but he had zoomed ahead, enjoying the sense of isolation.

> *"Snow fell early this morning and the landscape was like a Christmas card,"* he wrote. *"Just me and the road. My mind divided perfectly in two, half taken up with the beauty and half glued to the surface below me. A slip on one of those hairpin bends and I would have gone air-borne. So alive."*

That loner spirit still puzzled me, but here in Kalk Bay it no longer frustrated me. This time I didn't nag. Instead, I got my own bike – a gleaming baby-blue BMW, not as big as his but powerful enough for me.

Felix was angry. He sulked. All he would say was, "It's not a game, you silly woman. People get hurt on these things!"

Obviously, he wouldn't teach me, so I took lessons with an instructor. I was scared out of my gourd. When Gregory Szimansky arrived at the house on his machine, a gorgeous shiny red beast, I invited him in for tea, and asked how he got into this business and if he'd ever had any accidents – anything to keep him talking and delay the evil hour. But he was used to my kind. He had me sit on my bike for a long time, while he discussed each part, from the kickstand up. Then he made me crawl around it on my hands and knees, "so you can see what a bloody beautiful machine this is and how everything is connected."

Only then did he let me turn on the ignition. From the first *vvvrrrooom* I was hooked. In that instant, I was back to being that 21-year-old in her yellow sun dress, lusting after the guy straddling his Harley, or maybe just lusting after his bike. Demure little Bunnington craved speed – and this old dame was going to get her some.

It was a sparkling Cape Town day, the sunshine bright and the shadows sharp. We slowly cruised down our driveway, around the block, and back along the Main Road. Not exactly the Grand Prix, but enough to have my nerves on hyper alert, and to be embarrassed. It's a narrow street for the volume of traffic, trapped between the train line and shore on one side and the stores and houses on the other. A truck crawled behind me, patiently waiting, but horns tooted behind him, and it was a relief to turn into our side street.

Felix was waiting as we pulled into the driveway, his expression thunderous. He didn't say anything, just turned on his heel and stalked back inside. Had he been that scared? It was so unlike him to worry. I had a silent chuckle, relishing the fact that, for once, I'd freaked him out instead of the other way around.

The next twenty-four hours were the chilliest I'd ever experienced with Felix. He busied himself at his desk with I-don't-know-what, went for a long walk without inviting me, and went to bed early that night. He was asleep, or appeared to be, by the time I turned in. I didn't like it, but I wasn't perturbed. If he didn't want to tell me why it was such a big deal, well that was his problem. While he had worked and walked, I was paging through the big BMW manual the previous owner provided with my bike, trying to decipher the diagrams and master all these new terms.

And then, typically, Felix put aside his anger and got involved. The next morning, when I woke up he was already out of bed. I found him lying on the driveway, checking out the bike. "Just making sure," he said. "You probably paid too much, but it is in great shape."

A few weeks after I passed my test, we rode our bikes to a track on the other side of the city, and Felix began showing me more sophisticated techniques, how to sight your way through a curve, how to steer out of a skid. It was a gesture of respect that pleased me deeply. We rode home via De Waal Drive, with the city spread out below us. He led the way, showing me how to swoop in and out of the crawling lanes of cars.

"Remember riding in the snow in the States?" I asked when we were home at last, settled on the couch with two frosty beers. Years ago, in our phone calls between California and New York, he described riding through Colorado in winter, and across the bitter cold flatlands of Iowa. He went up to Alaska too in the early spring one year, riding through endless mud and slush.

"Why did you do it?" I asked then. Now I had a whole new appreciation of the challenge. It sounded awful — and wonderful.

He lit up at the memory. "Because around each bend the scenery got more beautiful. The sky and the water and the trees. I've never been dirtier, and I've never been happier on a bike." And in more detail than ever before, he told me about the routes, and the people, the near-disasters with passing trucks, and the fabulous fellowship encountered along the way.

Cape Town, thank goodness, wasn't as muddy or as icy, though the wind could be a challenge. We started going out together every few days, along the coast road to Simonstown and across the mountain to Hout Bay, along Chapman's Peak, that glorious winding route high above the ocean. He still headed off on his own every now and then, and I rode occasionally with people I met at a BMW owners' club — a group that didn't include Harley people like him — but most of it became a shared pleasure. Each on our own vehicle but joyfully together.

Till my knee got too sore. I sold my bike back in January,

with great reluctance, assuming I wouldn't be able to ride it again. Felix was riding his bike less too but wasn't about to give it up. And still, he wouldn't let me ride with him as a passenger.

Now the Harley is sitting out there, so forlorn. Seems like a waste.

~ 13 ~

Steps

S o, tell me," Felix's daughter says now, "How come you never had children?"

He asked that same question the next time we met face to face, twelve years after the Los Angeles encounter. We had stayed in touch, with occasional letters and now and then a phone call. He suggested emailing, and that gave me the inducement to master the technology, to the delight of colleagues who'd been nudging me in that direction without much success. Hard to imagine now how I ever lived without it. His emails always made me smile.

I wonder what my mother would have said about that connection, and this next get-together. She was gone by then, so I can only speculate. Imma went downhill so suddenly, I had no chance to say goodbye except over the phone, with a nurse holding the receiver to her ear. For months afterwards, years really, I continued to have conversations with her in my mind. When you know each other so well, why not? Through my worst times, she is still at my shoulder.

"Would Charles approve?" she'd have asked.

Pops followed her in less than a year. He didn't exactly commit suicide, but he faded so rapidly, it was obvious he didn't want to live without her. But at least I was able to be with him at the end, called back by a Cape Town friend who watched over him as his heart failed.

"Do not mourn for me, *meidele*," he insisted, his voice more air than tone. I tried to hush him, with that stupid notion that if he saved his breath, he could win more time. "I should have been dead in 1945. This has all been a bonus, all a blessing. But without my Irene, enough. I am tired. I am done."

Flying back from Cape Town, I kept thinking about the contrast between our marriage and my parents'. Would Charles want to die rather than live without me?

If an objective observer had peered in through a window of our home, they would have seen a happy enough tableau. As he had after the miscarriage, Charles supported me through my mourning, snuggling me to sleep at night, and coming home early from work – at least for the first few weeks. He had a photo of my parents enlarged and set in a beautiful hand-carved frame, and he took to making the coffee in the morning and bringing me a cup in bed. "How are you doing today?" he'd ask, and I'd snuggle down for an extra ten minutes before facing the world.

He also began spending more time at the gym, supposedly to give me more time for myself. "I know you need it," he said.

By the time I saw Felix in 1995, Charles and I were chugging along on parallel tracks, peacefully enough. Probably better than most of the marriages around us. We had a home we both loved. We went to synagogue services on the High Holy Days, cooked holiday meals together, played bridge with a few other couples, and subscribed to a concert series at the Met. As far as I knew, he hadn't strayed again, and I certainly hadn't.

It was what my friend Libby called "a solid foundation," on which she still hoped I would build a family like hers. But she was daydreaming about grandmotherhood, and I hadn't made it through the starting gate. Deep into my forties, I'd kept trying to fall pregnant, going for various treatments and more testing, always with outcomes just positive enough to keep me hoping. I nudged Charles every now and then to come with me for a consultation, but his father-the-doctor dismissed fertility specialists as quacks, so he did too. "I told you, I've been tested and everything's in order," he'd say. He optimized our chances, he'd tell me, by working out and avoiding tight underwear.

"Maybe you should go to the gym too," he'd say with a little smile.

Maybe I should. All those muscly young men, glistening with sweat might kickstart my ovaries, I thought. I didn't say it out loud. If he had said, "Come with me," I might have, but that wasn't what he suggested, and I had no desire to go alone.

"Well, you're going to be rich and famous," Libby said.

Not likely, though my career was going well. I was head of the music department, and my first book had just come out, *New Steps*. It outlined the work I'd been doing at the school and with groups in other communities around the U.S., finding the common elements between different traditions and enabling the children to create their own dances built on those links.

Charles was less intrigued with my teaching than he'd been with my performing, but it gave me immense joy. I'd walk into an unfamiliar studio and see two bunches of children from separate schools eyeing each other across the gleaming floor. Toes turned out, clad in black leotards and pink tights, or regular street clothes, they would frown at me as the unfamiliar music began to fill the room. Lights out, I'd start with a video to break the ice and show them some glorious ethnic dances from around the world. Murmurs turned to chatter, and then, with the lights back on, to questions and volunteering, as I invited them, two or three at a time, to come try some steps with me and one another.

Remembering, as I sit in my South African kitchen, chatting with Joanie, my knobby feet flex and point, and I seesaw my hips. She laughs and offers a harmonizing ripple of hands, like a hula dancer. She's seen a couple of my classes. By the end of a two-hour session, the kids would be swirling and swooping, hopping and stamping, arms stretching and weaving, all intermingled. I loved hearing the "Aaaaw!" in protest at the announcement that our time had come to an end.

But, yeah – fame was elusive. The book was a satisfying accomplishment, but no major publications had reviewed it, and the publisher was taking ages to get it into bookstores. Charles's mother was trying to work her high-society contacts to get me publicity, but it was slow going.

Felix's life seemed so much more exciting. I knew he had been in Japan and in Switzerland – that he'd spent time there with his friend Maria, and in South Africa, where he voted in the country's first democratic elections, and that a few years back in San Francisco, he'd linked up with that much younger woman and had a son. I knew just enough to see the outlines, like a map, without the details of his day-to-day endeavors.

Then he called out of the blue. It was a soggy October day. The house phone rang just as I walked in the door and shook out my umbrella. I shed my raincoat – the old red Paddington one still in service – as I reached for the phone, expecting to hear Charles, probably calling to let me know he'd be late again.

"Felix here. Hello, Copper Girl. How are you?"

It was so good to hear him. I flopped into the big armchair, put my feet up on the footstool and settled in to enjoy a catch-up session.

"I'm fine, I suppose. How are you? Where are you, my peripatetic friend?"

"I'm in New York," he said, "with my kids. Are you free tomorrow afternoon? Would you like to meet them?"

Answering Joanie's question about children, I feel my way through the thickets of memory, dodging what's still loaded while wanting to share as much as possible. "Remember the first time we met?" I ask, and her eyes go wide.

"At the Natural History Museum!" she exclaims. "I'd forgotten all about that. Dad brought us to New York on one of his work trips. Wasn't he giving a talk somewhere? And Nellie's sister Helen invited us to come stay with her. Do you remember those little animals you bought us? We each got to choose. I think Trevor wanted a black bear. I got the most beautiful glass antelope. I've still got it."

It pleases me that she remembers that day with such warmth. For me it was a mixture, the beginning of my friendship with the kids, and the start of a very dark chapter in my life.

My knee had been giving me trouble, still stiff after an accident in jazz class. Spending way too many hours at a desk, working on my magnum opus, hadn't helped, but given Charles's much more serious issues, worsening as he got older, I was doing my best to ignore it and hoped it would heal on its own. I walked into the cafeteria at the museum, trying to look light on my feet, my hair shoulder-length and curling way out of control and faded to pale peach. Definitely not his copper dancer anymore.

Felix didn't seem to notice. He leapt up from his chair and came towards me with outstretched arms, his face alight with pleasure. We hugged, and he turned and introduced me to Joanie and Trevor. I could see a glimmer of that tiger-kitten look in her, but she was a gangly teenager already, shy and awkward until we warmed to each other.

Trevor was bouncing up and down wanting to go see other displays. He wasn't interested in meeting this stranger, but I couldn't take my eyes off him. He had yellow-brown eyes like his dad's, tight brass-colored curls and caramel skin. I hadn't a clue -- until that moment -- that Felix's Nellie was not a white

Jamaican. He'd never said a word about her race.

Things with Trevor improved abruptly when I invited him to choose an animal in the gift store. He decided I was okay and turned on the charm, including me in his campaign to find monsters.

The interaction took me by surprise. For a long time after the miscarriage, I'd found it hard to be around other people's children, except at work. My Leila ghost still hovered. But these kids were so curious and enthusiastic and funny, they charmed me within minutes.

We had a wonderful time – until Trevor disappeared. One minute he had his nose pressed to the glass of a diorama, and the next he was gone. Joanie and I had been examining a display of hunting implements right next to him, while Felix read the explanatory text out loud to us. He turned to explain something to Trevor, and I heard him gasp, "Where the…?" We spun like three dreidels, each scanning frantically up the long, gleaming hall.

Cold shivers rippled over me. "Kidnapped!" "Abducted!" "Taken!" My old paranoia about people vanishing merged with memories of tabloid headlines. Joanie started shouting, "Trev, Trevor, TREVOR!" louder and even louder, her pitch rising. An attendant came striding over, tried to hush her, and asked me what was happening. I struggled to describe this small boy in orange pants and… What color was his jacket? Felix called details over his shoulder as he bobbed and ducked, trying to see between the legs of the coming and going people, up over a plinth, down under a display case.

"You need to go to the office and ask them to broadcast a

missing-child message," the attendant said. He was straight-faced, not unkind but clearly accustomed to these panics. I found his indifference calming, but it infuriated Felix.

He yelled at the man, "YOU tell the office! I can't walk away from here, from where he knows to find me." I'd never seen him so white-hot intense. I offered to go while he and Joanie kept searching that area, and we agreed where to reconnect.

I ran down the hall and up the great marble staircase, only vaguely aware of the twinges in my knee. As I reached the upper level, a woman wearing an official-looking blazer came striding by, scanning the room from side to side and dipping her head to the golden child beside her. He was chatting away, trying to show her his animal, and not in the least bit perturbed. I waylaid her and grasped Trevor's hand.

Felix had seen us from below. He bounded up the stairs, taking them two at a time, and grabbed the child from me, hugging him against his shoulder, rocking in silence. Joanie had run up too and now she sagged beside them like a rag doll. I gave her a squeeze and she grinned at me, sniffling and happy.

Adult Joanie heads out for a hike up the mountain, and I take the opportunity to do some exercises. Gradually, I'm growing a little looser, a little stronger. Then I clean up the kitchen and straighten the lounge, caring for this Cape Town home that has become so dear to me, while my thoughts rove back to that other home and other life.

At the time, I took its stability for granted. Looking back, the smooth façade was traced with cracks I should have spotted. I remember reading about the technique where instead of glazing over fractures in their pots, Japanese ceramicists fill them with gold. I was more into the glazing-over approach.

∽

Around four o'clock, Felix and I dropped the children off at their aunt's apartment, in time for her to take them to a matinee of *Babe*. Helen invited us to come too, but I was exhausted, hobbling, and not into seeing a movie about a pig, however articulate. I thought Felix might want to go with them rather than let Trevor out of his sight, but he was totally back to normal and insisted on walking me home.

We hovered in front of my building, still deep in conversation, each with a hand resting on the concrete lion guarding the steps. He said, "Remember how you used to panic when I went off on my own without telling you? You know, I wasn't getting up to anything nefarious." I laughed and shrugged. Like father, like son, maybe.

Spatters of rain began dotting our clothes, and I invited him in. "If you've got time, come see my abode. I can make us tea, South African style, with scones, like we used to have. I baked some yesterday."

It was an innocent invitation. After the initial hug, we hadn't touched one another all day, though our eyes met a few times over the kids' heads. Walking along the street, our hands brushed once or twice, but didn't clasp. Still, my heart thumped waiting for his answer.

"I'd love to see your abode. Will Charles be home soon? I'd like to meet him."

I was pretty sure Charles wouldn't be back till much later. He seemed to be in a rhythm of having an early dinner with colleagues and then going back to work for a couple of hours. "That way I come home ready to relax, with a free conscience," he said. I didn't mention that to Felix. Whether for my sake or his, it seemed wiser to keep open the possibility of being interrupted.

I flicked on the lights and ushered him in with pride. The apartment looked warm and inviting. "Charles and I bought this place three years ago," I told him. "It used up all my savings and put us in debt to his family, but we love it."

Given my reluctance to rely on his parent's money, we probably should have stayed put where we were, renting on East 76th Street. But after I injured my knee, the climb to the fourth floor had become a daily strain. Loath as he was to admit it, Charles was having trouble with the climb too. When one of their cousins offered us this beautiful place in an elevator building he owned in the Village, we couldn't resist. Charles's folks cosigned the lease and undertook to cover a third of our monthly payment, brushing it off as an advance on his inheritance. That bothered me, but I loved the place.

I left Felix in the living room and went to make the tea. He came strolling through a few minutes later and, at my urging, peered out the back window. It was the kind of view outsiders don't associate with New York – an expanse of back gardens with big trees and, in summer, a patchwork of flowers. Now the green branches were dotted with the first flares of yellow and orange. He opened the window wide and sniffed in the moist air, and then turned back and, with a querying look, asking permission, began to examine our array of handmade mugs and my collection of oddball tea pots. His curiosity pleased me. He asked about some of them and then pointed to the homely brown pot I'd just filled. It was like one we had in Grahamstown. I nodded without a word, knowing what he was thinking, and lifted the tea tray. He took it from me and carried it into the living room.

"When I first lived in the city," I told him, "I would walk past homes like this at night, spying through the windows and seeing the golden glow and the shelves laden with books. I wondered who lived in such places and if they knew how fortunate they were."

Our shelves were packed with Charles's collection of books and records and mine, interspersed with our respective treasures – an antique globe, a miniature bronze of Degas's little dancer, framed pictures of his parents and mine. The lighting came from the Tiffany lamps.

Felix said, "This place is wonderful, Sal. It has your vibe."

My fatigue had vanished, and everything was giving me pleasure: the fragrance of the tea, the light gleaming off the furniture, the beloved face in front of me. I showed him my book in its glossy cover. He turned it in his hands and exclaimed, "Sally, this is just fantastic. I am so proud of you. It looks absolutely wonderful." He read the cover copy and paged through the opening, pausing to examine some of the photographs of dancing children, and we reminisced about the kids I taught in Grahamstown.

I asked about his work and, as he answered, poured the tea and buttered a scone for him, scooping on a dollop of apricot jam. Between crumbly mouthfuls, he tried to condense what he was doing in layman terms, and I more or less managed to follow. It dealt with encouraging the body to regain muscle and nerve function, using electrical stimulation, but mostly through patterns of pressure and release, he said.

He told me anecdotes about his colleagues, and I compared them to some of mine. We were back into shorthand, as if we'd never been apart, darting from topic to topic, one idea opening up another.

For all my best resolutions, the energy lighting up my brain lit up my skin as well. I wanted to feel his hair, long and disheveled again like when we first met, now receding at the temples. My eyes kept fixing on his hands, on the square finger tips, on the ridges of tendon and vein on the backs. I wanted to stroke them, but this time I didn't.

Felix went silent. He looked into my face, his eyes scanning from feature to feature and resting on my lips. He whispered: "I'm having trouble keeping my hands to myself, but I know if I touch you, I won't stop. May I touch you?"

My hand lay on the cushion an inch from his. I dragged it back, and groaned, "No. Don't. You're married, committed to Nellie. I'm married. I hated myself for what happened last time. Whatever was going on between you and Deidre, or what's happening with you and Nellie now, it's not how I want to conduct myself."

He nodded. "I know you felt bad last time, Sal. It made me sad. It was so wonderful." He stuck his hands beneath his thighs, as if to keep them under control, and grinned at me like a naughty kid. "It was good, wasn't it?"

He asked me about kids. And finally, I described what had

happened after I got back to New York, about the pregnancy and the miscarriage. The memory had been filed so deep inside me, it was hard to cloak in words.

He kept saying, "Oh, God, I'm so, so sorry. I wish you'd let me know. I should have been there for you."

"But it might have been Charles's."

He grabbed my hands. "I wouldn't have loved the child any less. If I could have been with you, I wouldn't have cared if it was his or mine. There was no deception between you and me. We should have been together." And then he shook his head as if waking up, realizing. "Oh, of course. There was Charles. And I had Joanie. Is he good to you?"

I told him about Charles's affair from that same time. He snorted. "Ha, so that's why you were so willing to be with me. I wondered — but I wasn't about to say anything that might give you second thoughts. You stayed with him…?"

I told him how hard Charles worked to make up for what he'd done, and how caring he was after the miscarriage.

"And since then?" he asked

"We've been all right. He's a good guy, and we have a pleasant life together." He raised his eyebrows, unimpressed. "It's okay. I adore his family. So no complaints. But no luck on the baby front. There were a few hopeful moments, times when I was a few days overdue, but nothing really. And now, of course, it's probably way too late."

He gently stroked my hair back behind my shoulder. "Adoption?"

"I thought of it, but Charles refuses. He says we'd never know what genetic background the kid might have. I don't know why that matters, but he's adamant. He wants his own, or none."

"I shouldn't pass judgment," Felix said. "What I feel for my kids goes beyond anything I ever imagined, and I know part of that is biology, seeing my own genes in them. But it's a pity. You would make a wonderful mother."

We had slowly moved closer, and his arm was around my shoulders. I lay two fingers against his cheek and drew them under the curve of his lower lip, mesmerized. He leaned in closer, lips parted – and I jerked back.

"No. I said no. I mean no."

Felix pulled back too. He said, "I don't know if this makes any difference, but you should know Nellie and I have an understanding. For the first time in my life, I have an absolutely honest, two-way agreement that we can each do as we please."

Longing and indignation mixed and ignited. "That's bullshit. Don't tell me she's fine with you falling into bed with whoever takes your fancy! I've never ever come across a woman who'd be all right with that. It's a myth you men make up to make yourselves feel better."

I stood up. It wasn't that I wanted him to leave, but I needed to distance myself, to hold onto that anger. He rose too, scowling, and grabbed me by the shoulders. "For your information, Miss Know-it-all, it was her idea – and it's Nellie who's gone off with whoever, not me. That's the fine irony of this; finally, free – and not interested in freedom. I really haven't wanted to screw anyone else – till now, with you."

We stared at each other, both seething, then slowly simmered down. I put my arms around his waist. He wrapped his around me, and we just stood there, stymied.

"I want so much to be naked and entangled with you," I said finally. "But I won't betray my vows again."

As he stood back, his hands trailing down my arms and away, it was as if the skeins of longing had taken solid form. I could almost see them, and there was no telling on which side they began or ended.

He put on his jacket and slung his scarf around his neck, and we walked to the door. *I'm still in love with you,* I wanted to say. I tugged the ends of the scarf and then released them. *Always will be.*

~ 14 ~

Babies

Eric and the kittens arrive on the same day.

That synchronicity delights Joanie. It's as if all parts of her light up.

Through the fog of sleep, I hear an odd, low yowling. I shuffle out of bed and in the direction of the sound but can't see Mergatroid. Joanie emerges from the spare room and spots the white tip of a tail visible under the table. On our knees in the semi-darkness, we see her lying in the box of Felix's sweaters that I stashed away in a hurried attempt to tidy the room the day before. I get a flashlight and try not to shine it directly into the box. Mergatroid turns her yellow eyes to us and goes back to licking a little dark sausage that's starting to wiggle. And then she goes very still, and from her nether end another sausage emerges with a spill of liquid. She ends up with four babies, two vaguely gray and white, two orange and white, squeaking and nudging at her belly.

All these new beings in this home where this morning it was just us. Joanie and I finally settle down with our first cups of coffee, high on the miracle of life.

"Cheers, Grandma," Joanie says, lifting her mug. "To life and the pursuit of happiness."

"What about liberty?" I ask. She is grinning at me. "Life, liberty, and the pursuit..."

"You gotta be kidding!" Joanie exclaims. "She's pinned down for the duration. She's not going to have liberty again for at least two months, or whenever you manage to find homes for that lot."

"You sound a little vehement. That's how you feel about motherhood?"

Joanie chuckles and brings over the coffee pot to give us refills. "Actually, I wasn't going to say anything until Eric was here too. We wanted to tell you together. But seeing as how you've put me on the spot, I'm three-and-a-half months in. But at least I'm only expecting one, not four, and Eric has vowed he'll do his part!"

I hug her hard, my head swirling with emotion. Maybe it's the combined impact of Mergatroid's delivery and this news. I'm so happy. And in that moment so sad. "I wish your dad was here for this," I sniff. "He would have danced a jig around the kitchen."

Joanie reaches for a tissue. "Me too. He would have made

the most wonderful, eccentric grandpa. But maybe this baby will have some of his personality. You know what they say about souls coming and going?"

I confess how I've been wanting to ask her about babies but was scared. "And your coffee consumption made me think it wasn't on the cards just yet."

"My doctor says it's okay," Joanie says. "Only two cups a day. It's my one vice."

She looks at me, smiling, and then her expression goes grim. "You know, you're happier about this than my mother. The first words out of her mouth were, 'I'm too young to be a grandmother.' She's such a bitch! Generous with money but clueless when it comes to mothering. I just hope to heck I'm not like her with my kids."

"You won't be," I say, though I don't really know her mom. I do know Joanie. "You will be fabulous."

We leave Mergatroid in peace a few hours later and walk to the station to meet Eric. Resourceful fellow, he'd insisted on getting a bus from the airport to Cape Town city center and a suburban train from there. It's just whooshed out of the station as we get there and he's standing alone on the platform with his bag at his feet, the other passengers already making their way under the train tracks to the beach or the opposite way to the road. It's so much quieter than in the summer, though there are more commuters than just a few years ago.

He gives me a hug first, and then turns to Joanie, holding her at arm's length, looking her over and drinking in the sight, before he takes her into a long embrace. It's good to see. He's a self-contained kind of person, sturdy and very deliberate in his movements, and last time we met on their previous trip, it worried me that he wasn't very demonstrative. But things have evolved between them. They look like a couple, soon to be a family. She must have just told Eric that she spilled the beans, because he casts me a grin and gives her belly a possessive circular stroke.

This baby stuff is stirring old thoughts, long buried. Joanie seems to have forgotten her question, but I haven't. She heads out into the sunshine with her man, and my mind turns back to New York, the memories limned with a sharp edge of anger and regret.

∽

I intended to tell Charles about Felix's visit after the Natural History Museum, simply because it seemed right. The apartment was his home as well as mine, and there had been this other person in it. He knew a bit about Felix, that we'd been involved way back in college, that he worked in medical research and we kept in touch, but he hadn't shown any curiosity about him. I knew way more about his romantic history, his first love, the girl who broke his heart in college, the one he married briefly in grad school, etc., etc. What Charles didn't tell me his mother did, generally by way of letting me know I was a great improvement on all of them.

Still I would have told him, were it not for his dark mood when he finally got home. I'd phoned his office to ask when he'd be back. Dorothea, his assistant, said he'd just left. She sounded irritated – though I couldn't tell if it was because of something he'd done, or with me for further delaying her exit from the office. I decided it had to be annoyance with him and his moodiness.

He walked in half an hour later, tossed his wet coat on the corduroy couch, and asked what was for dinner. I picked the coat up and hung it on the coat stand. "What's for dinner? You haven't eaten dinner here on a week night in months!"

"So, don't you eat? Aren't you buying food anymore? Just because I'm working late doesn't mean I don't sometimes come home hungry."

It was such a gratuitous attack, it dawned on me that something was amiss. "Are you all right?"

"Why wouldn't I be?"

He opened the liquor cabinet and poured himself a whisky neat. Usually, he poured for me too and added water to both. That's how he'd been advised to drink it at an adult school course taught by some famous Scots whisky blender, and he had done so ever since. He didn't even offer me any. And right then I didn't want to drink with him.

But maybe he was ratty because he was hungry. I got out some takeout menus – Chinese, Mexican, Italian, Thai. "Shall we order something? Or would you like to go somewhere?" Venturing out into the cold and rain was decidedly unappealing, but it seemed a way to improve the atmosphere.

He stared blankly at me, and then said, "Yes, let's go out. Maybe that's a good idea."

We walked, or rather I limped, and he lurched up the avenue to our regular Thai restaurant. His balance was always worse if he was distracted or upset, but once we were seated in the mellow inner sanctum, I thought he'd relax.

The one good thing I can say about Charles, he was always

a good conversationalist. In all our years together there'd never been a time when he didn't have something he wanted to talk about. I could participate if I wanted; if I was in a quiet mood or it was an unfamiliar topic, I could rely on him to hold forth in a happy monolog. And the man was smart enough, and so lively-minded, that it was always interesting.

But he sat eating in silence, munching his way through a large chicken stir-fry. I'd ordered the same dish and knew how spicy it was, but he kept upping the ante with more sauce and another sprinkle of pepper. It was as if he was trying to block out any other awareness inside him. I tried to initiate conversation, but when I asked about his day, he looked up in irritation as if I'd interrupted his train of thought. I was going to tell him about going to the museum and losing Trevor, and about the latest sales figures on my book that had come in a day or two before, but that urge withered. I didn't know when last we'd spoken very much about anything.

We ate, paid, and went home and to bed without touching or exchanging more than necessities. I wasn't worried so much as annoyed with Charles for being unpleasant. In the morning, calmer and more focused, I remembered that the previous day was the anniversary of the death of one of his childhood friends, his *yahrzeit*. I apologized and kissed him on the cheek. He nodded, acknowledged he'd been grumpy, and said, "It just reminds me that I'm getting older and life's passing, and there's so much I haven't experienced yet."

I'm getting older too, I thought, *and this self-centeredness is getting old too.* Perhaps I should step up my yoga practice or join the women's group my friend Anne swore by. "We vent, we drink, we go home happy," she told me. Not quite my scene but learning to vent in a safe place might be just what I needed. A therapist would have suggested I vent to Charles himself, but I wasn't in therapy.

Felix called me the next day, just to say the kids loved meeting me, and he was really glad we'd had that time together.

"It was a special day," he said.

"Even though...?"

"Even though."

Over the next few weeks Charles was still distracted and terse. When I asked if something else was wrong, he insisted all was fine. I should have been more persistent, but I found myself welcoming his bad behavior. It gave me an excuse to ignore him.

And I had a distraction of my own. Felix was calling me at work and emailing every few days. Nothing long, just staying in touch for the pleasure of exchanging news and views. We seemed to have elevated the link between us – from *eros* to *philia* – but with a new intensity. He made it clear that he thought I was the cat's whiskers. And that made me purr. Across the width of the continent, having behaved so well, I felt free to adore him too.

But, of course, with that came guilt. Good wives don't dote on other men. They focus on their mates, not old boyfriends. I again started wearing the diamond engagement ring Charles gave me way back in our courting days, though it was a bit tight. I'd taken it off because of horror stories of robberies on the subway. "You could get your finger hacked off for that ring," one of my colleagues had said, "especially if they can't get it off easily." Well, maybe that was a risk I needed to take. He was my life partner, come what may.

And Felix had his partner, whom I respected. He and I talked about having dinner together, the four of us, if they came to New York. I wanted to be able to face Nellie with equanimity, clear that I had no designs on her man. I even asked Felix when her birthday was and — with his permission — sent her a card I made with the photo I'd taken of Felix and the kids at the museum. She sent an enthusiastic thank you note, saying she looked forward to meeting me. The guilt deepened.

And then suddenly the Felix-Charles tension resolved itself. Music has always unfurled my thinking. Listening to an inspired performance of Verdi's *La Traviata*, sitting alongside my handsome husband and his parents in a box at Lincoln Center, with the voices rising in a glorious crescendo, the realization dawned: I could love that person from my youth without taking anything away from this relationship, in the same way that I had room in my heart for both my mother and my father, or for class after class of students. *Love isn't restricted like a fist-sized heart; it's as wide as the sky*, I thought.

As it happens, the inspiration that evening came from a story all about ill-fated love. The heroine dies and the curtain falls. That part I ignored. I was feeling noble.

About a month after the museum day, the Wednesday before Thanksgiving, Felix called me at work and said he had been reading *New Steps*. I was packing up to go home, but I settled back at my desk. "It's beautifully done," he said. I waited for more. There was a hesitation in his voice. "What's here is fascinating, and you've laid it out very clearly. I'm knocked out by how many places you've been, and taught, and the way you use culture to connect the kids to these broader concepts."

"But — something's bothering you. What did I leave out?"

"Ha, you still read me better than anyone else. It's not that you left anything out; it's just that there's so much more that could be included. I know you have more to say. There isn't enough of Sally Paddington in here." I told him it was commissioned, and my goal was to convey the theory in a way other teachers could use.

"Fair enough. But you should do another book," he said. "I'm going to nag you until you do it."

We didn't go much further, but the possibility was invigorating. I did have all sorts of ideas and memories that could be fun to explore. The buzz from that conversation buoyed my spirits all the way home on the subway, through the cold, darkening day. There had been an early snowfall in the afternoon, just enough to leave a layer of crunchy froth on the top of the garbage baskets and benches and along the branches of the trees lining our block. The city looked festive, and I felt that way too, frothy and bright.

Charles was home early and was in the kitchen, cooking. He didn't seem to be working late anymore, and I'd been careful to stock up on fresh ingredients and a stash of ready-to-eat dishes. I'd even made a quart of his favorite spicy sauerkraut with caraway seeds, just the way Imma taught me.

I shed my outer layers and joined him. It was the first time in ages I'd made it all the way home without noticing my knee.

And we had a pleasant prospect ahead. It was a four-day weekend and his family had a grand reunion planned, starting with the Thanksgiving Day feast, with cousins coming in from far and wide.

Perched on a stool by the counter, I said, "Guess what, my old friend Felix suggested I do another book, expanding on the topics I covered in *New Steps* in a more personal way. I think it could be a lot of fun to do."

I thought he'd be enthusiastic, given how much he used to enjoy watching me dance and still sometimes enjoyed seeing my students. But he turned to me with his thick black brows bunched like storm clouds and a sneer I'd never seen before.

"Your old friend Felix? Are you seriously expecting me to get all happy and excited that you and that fellow are cooking up plans together? He's the one, isn't he?"

I sat down at the kitchen table, winded. "The one what? What on earth are you angry about?"

"You have the damn nerve to ask that?" he yelled. "You think you can make an idiot of me forever?"

Darkness veiled my brain. I went blank. And then that restaurant patio in Los Angeles flickered into view. And the pregnancy that followed. And my confusion. How the hell did he know about L.A.?

There was no chance to find out. And I'm not sure how hard I would have tried anyway. All the air had gone out of my lungs. No words and no energy. He glared at me, then grabbed the pan he'd been cooking with and tossed the contents into the garbage can.

His voice — a-usually so mellifluous — was hoarse. He said,

"I can't stay in this place with you. I'm going to Connecticut to my folks. I'd appreciate it if you moved out before I get back on Sunday night."

❧

Wondering again why, when so much of life disappears from our thoughts as fast as water on hot sand, certain events get engraved indelibly in our brains. There are so many days I would far rather recall than that horrible Wednesday night, but they've faded away. Retrievable maybe with the right stimuli, like the nerve impulses Felix's gadgets would seek to revive, to get muscles functioning again?

Thinking of him and how passionately he wanted to help the disabled soothes my roiled mood. His achievements were wonderful and deserved to be known and celebrated by a far wider audience. I wish I'd helped bring him that glory.

~ *15* ~

Homes

The kids from next door come over to see Mergatroid's litter. The eldest, a seven-year-old who takes her big-sister duties very seriously, keeps telling the bouncing five-year-old to "cool it or you'll scare the kittens" and catches her three-year-old brother's hands just before they can grab a squirmy little body. "I told you, no touching, Bennie, or you can't come see them again."

Truth is the kittens are not all that interesting yet. They just squirm and suck, and peer about with their milky, just-opened eyes. How strange and baffling this world must be. And yet within weeks they will be mastering a hundred skills, climbing and stalking and catching. "Then they'll be lots of fun," I tell Samantha.

She looks up at me from under her blond fringe accusingly: "But will you still be here?"

"Why? What have you heard?" An inappropriate question to ask the child, but she has caught me off guard. Joanie, just in from a jaunt to the supermarket, evidently hears the question, and my response. She stops in her tracks, eyebrows raised, waiting for the next line.

Sam says, "Mommy said now that Uncle Felix is dead you won't want to live here anymore. She said other people will come to live here." She scowls at me as if I've betrayed her, and the other two cluster next to her, confused, but joining forces.

"Maybe the new people will have children," I say lamely. "You might prefer having them rather than an old lady like me as a neighbor."

I see the kids back through the gap in the hedge and return to the kitchen. Joanie has dumped her bags on the table and flopped down on a chair, catching her breath. She still looks slim but now that I know, I can see she's feeling the impact of the pregnancy.

"Is that what you're planning to do?" she asks.

"Do?"

"Move out. So you're planning to leave? Where are you going? What are we meant to do with the place? We don't have enough time to sell it now." To my astonishment, she starts crying, not in a dramatic way but with tears sliding down her cheeks. It's probably the hormones.

Were it not for the tears, I might try to answer more circumspectly, but I hurry to assure her. "Everything's going to be fine. The selling will be easy. I'll handle it if you can't. A couple of agents have already been in touch. You should meet with them. They say the market is very good. This little old house will fetch quite a packet – enough to give you help with buying a place of your own in California – or starting a college fund for the baby."

"We don't need help buying a place," she says. "We're doing okay. So's Trevor. But, fine, if you're in such a hurry, we'll talk to the real estate agents." Joanie takes her shoulder bag and stalks out, and I hear the spare room door bang shut.

My heart is thumping again, but not with excitement like when she mentioned us doing a dance. I'm utterly unaccustomed to this kind of intimate conflict. With Felix, despite the no-go areas I didn't touch, with something like this I would have said, "What the fuck is wrong?" and he would probably have told me. In recent years, I've learned to be more that way with friends too – instead of simply withdrawing and hoping it all blows over. But this girl's vulnerability gets right under my ribs. I can't get angry with her or frosty, and I have no clue what upset her. Instead an anger rises at Felix for not being here to mediate.

For the first time in a while, I put on my used-to-be-blue hat and a jacket and head out the door for a walk. I need to move and move fast.

I'm so tired of the anxieties bottled up inside me. I don't want Joanie and Eric to leave. I don't want to leave. I don't want to go back to being the "soloist" I used to be. That was Libby's word for me, way back when I first landed in Boston. The dancer in me liked it, but she didn't mean it as a positive. She couldn't understand how anyone could live so far away from family, but then she had about six hundred cousins and nieces and nephews. I wanted relatives too. Thought I'd found them with Charles.

My back is spasming and I do my best to push through the pain, to force it to relax. Action thoughts. Positive thoughts. Walking and planning, breathing deep. When the kids are gone, I'll get serious about clearing out and making the place shipshape, ready to sell. I have to hurry before the next round of rates and taxes fall due. But it shouldn't be a problem. It's true the house should sell quickly.

Where am I going to go? I've paged idly through the real estate pages of the newspaper Joanie brought home. The cottages in my price range aren't anywhere close to the ocean. What is in my range are condos in new developments, those cutesy cheek-by-jowl places that are springing up like mushrooms further inland.

Depression comes swirling in over the rocks like a returning tide, carrying bits of old debris, reminders of other times, other dislocations. The exhaust from cars crawling along the main road intersperses with a fishy smell from the harbor and then wafts of fresh ocean breeze. I could go back to America and reclaim my little Brooklyn flat. But then I'd lose that monthly income, and it would feel so cramped after this. Even if I sell it and move to Jersey City or Hoboken, I won't find anything larger than a mouse trap. And having put down roots here again, going back to being a foreigner would rankle.

I'm cold at first and achy. But the day is bright, and the waves are jumping, filling my eyes with blue and white movement. Within half an hour, I'm feeling warmer and looser, and more serene. On my inner movie screen, some intriguing dynamics begin emerging, interweaving to a range of rhythms — a thump-thump of Zulu, a swirl of flamenco, some samba. Fancy footwork for Felix, the lover of dancers? Not sure how many shape shifters it involves, two or three or four.

$\backsim$

"My husband discovered I slept with someone else years before," I tell Joanie the next day. This openness doesn't come easily to me, but there's still a lingering tension with her. I don't understand what upset her, and I desperately want to re-establish the bond between us. "He divorced me."

She and I are up in the attic, and she has repeated her question about my past. It sounded a bit aggressive — as if she's become suspicious about my priorities, and I want to answer her properly. Half the time, she is glued to the open window, taking photographs instead of working. Well, I suppose this is her work, and the vista is even more spectacular than usual, with dark and light clouds massed in teetering towers.

Last year, she published a magnificent book on hiking trails in Oregon, and she's been muttering about doing a book about "exploring roots." We've had some wonderful discussions about books and how to find one's topic and one's market. It's reminded me that not so long ago, I was passionately pursuing a market for my own work. Meanwhile, she is still doggedly pursuing answers, and I'm battling to edit as I talk, to divulge only what is my business and not Felix's.

She casts a glance over her shoulder. "That doesn't seem your style. Dad always said you were one of the most moral people he knew. Was it just a casual fling?"

"Oh, no. I'd been mad about this man – and we met up again by chance, right at a very vulnerable moment."

"And that's why Charles dumped you? How did he find out so much later?"

"I had no idea. It drove me nuts trying to work it out, but he was right, and I felt terrible about how much it was hurting him. I'd always wanted to avoid that."

Joanie listens without saying much. She isn't looking into my eyes the way she usually does. I've given so little thought to her mother, but maybe this is a Deidre effect, a wariness of getting too close to a maternal figure who might prove untrustworthy. It's a fear I can understand – though my own mother was very different – but what have I done to make her fear that from me? For all this time, through her teens and twenties and into her thirties, we've been friends. It's true, though, that with her father around I took a back seat. We never talked the way we have this time. It's pushing boundaries.

With miserable thoughts of Manhattan crowding my brain, it dawns on me that having to pack up this dear house is even harder than expected not just because there's so much stuff, not just because my heart is raw, but because of old scars.

That weekend when Charles was in Connecticut, I moved out as he'd requested, in fact the next day. I should have waited and packed properly or refused to go at all. Even in his absence, the rooms echoed with his words, filled with loathing. I couldn't bear to be there.

In desperation, I called Libby and asked if I could come to them up in Riverdale. Memories of Sunday lunches with her tumultuous household glowed in my brain. It would be the perfect distraction, and I could make myself useful. She apologized, saying she and her husband were going away for a kid-free anniversary celebration, but I could come after the weekend if I wanted. She began to ask why I needed a place to stay, but I made an excuse and rang off before she heard the hysteria tightening my voice.

Next, I called my colleague Sherrie. She lived alone in a huge apartment, the one she grew up in, and she'd had a note on the staffroom notice board advertising for a roommate. She chirped in delight at the prospect of company and insisted I stay as long as I wanted. In the end I was there for four months, until I found my little place in Brooklyn.

That Thursday morning, huddled like a mouse, I rode the uptown bus with my overnight bag clutched on my lap. Everyone else was heading to Thanksgiving get-togethers, and I was going to Sherrie and her cat. Little and gray and withdrawn. Felix's "Copper Girl" – ha! I kept thinking of Charles at his parents' place, so disillusioned, sure that his disciplined, demure wife was a slut. Passengers came and went in the aisle, squeezing past me, sitting opposite, getting on and off, and each one had eyes that could have seen me flirting at that sunny restaurant in California, or leaving hand-in-hand with Felix, heading to my hotel, carnal intent bright as paint on our faces.

I told Sherrie what had happened with Charles, and way back with Felix – the whole story. It gushed out. She was only the second person I'd ever confessed it to. She was shocked, and, to my annoyance, titillated. "You come over so proper," she giggled. "Who'd have thought you were having lurid affairs!"

"It happened once!" I bleated. "That's not even one affair." She had given me her best guest room. The four-poster bed had a gold-painted headboard and a frilly purple spread, like teenager princess décor. Sherrie curled up at the end of the bed, agog for more details, and I had none. "I've been faithful all these years. He slept with that student of his more times. That was an affair." She disappeared to the pantry and came back with a box of macaroons, and we nibbled and nattered all afternoon.

By the time Monday morning rolled around and we walked into the school together, I was pouting like a petulant child, cloyed with her caring. Sherrie promised not to breathe a word to anyone, but she was so bright-eyed, it took two minutes for the staff in the music department to find out I was staying with her. They wanted to know the reasons for my move, and when neither of us was forthcoming, they began throwing out guesses. I went into a cocoon. Even with people who'd been my buddies, I found it impossible to chit-chat about the breakup.

There was one person I wanted to talk to about it. Next to my fantasy princess bed in Sherrie's place there was a blue and mauve phone. It sat there at night, after things had gone quiet in the apartment and I was sure of my privacy. Given the three-hour time difference, Felix would probably be home, relaxing for the evening. He would be shocked and sympathetic and would remind me that I deserved to be loved. But what would Nellie make of that?

My intentions didn't feel as innocent as that pretty implement. I never used it.

Instead, I stewed in a bubbling mix of my own emotions. Being the baddie was a new role. No longer the *eshet chayil*, in the weeks that followed I slithered in and out of the condo, picking up one load of belongings at a time, hoping each time that I wouldn't bump into neighbors. When Charles and I crossed paths, my mood switched. I got indignant and tried to make my case that he should move, not me. He was the one who wanted out of our marriage. But he was adamant, and his disgust paralyzed me.

"You're the one who screwed up," he said, almost gleefully. He didn't say it, but I knew he was also thinking about the money his parents had put into the place.

You screwed up too, I wanted to shout, but he'd had the decency to confess his dalliance, where I'd preserved my image as the holier-than-thou wounded wife. And now I couldn't bring myself to admit to that hypocrisy. There's no way he'd buy my excuse that I stayed silent to spare his feelings. That fact sat like cotton fluff in my mouth.

He told his parents I cheated on him; that was the worst part. At the same time that I lost my marriage and my home, I also lost them, and his siblings, and his cousins, and the wonderful get-togethers. A few called me to express their regret, but all were clear that family loyalty came first. I considered calling his mother but feared she would slam down the phone. Finally, I wrote her a note, simply saying that I was terribly sorry about what had happened and hoping we could stay in touch. Ethel never replied.

A month into my stay with Sherrie, I was called in to the principal's office. The head of the arts department was there and two of the guidance counselors. They're all people I'd liked, and I started to smile until I registered their expressions.

"We have to let you go," the principal said.

The harsh sunlight flooding through the tall windows of her office cast everything into contrasts as sharp as a medieval woodcut. I sat there, speechless. "Please believe me, Sally, it's no reflection on you," she said. "You're a superb teacher. But we have no choice; we have to reduce our staffing." It didn't help. I felt like the gates of heaven had slammed shut and I was winding deeper into purgatory.

Money, never much of a concern in my life, became an obsession. The cost of subway tokens loomed large against the allure of Starbucks coffee. The digits of my bank balance flickered like stock prices across my brain, each down tick cause for another surge of panic. The pink porcelain piggy bank in a Chinese gift store window caught my eye. If I'd had one of those as a child, if my parents had been less indulgent and pushed me harder, perhaps I'd have saved more as a wife and been better prepared for this launch into the void.

In the heat of that anxiety, I took the biggest risk of my life. Perhaps I should have waited until the divorce was settled or I had a solid job, but camping at Sherrie's was becoming intolerable. I needed a base, a serene space of my own where I could unbox my books and set out my tea pots. I cashed in some of the bonds in South Africa purchased by my parents when I was a kid, added them to a loan from Libby and her husband, and bought the one-bedroom garden apartment in

Brooklyn.

It was down three moss-covered steps, but on a safe enough street with a couple of valiant trees, and two blocks from the subway. It was also damp and beset with mice. I gave up trying to trap them and started giving them names. There was Silver, and Sneak, and a fat one called Rollo. Rain water seeped in under the door, and the couple next door yelled a lot, in rage and lust and youthful enthusiasm.

That's when I began developing carpentry skills. To block the sound, I put up a false wall and built a loft bed that opened up a bit more floor space. For $30, the brawny son of the corner grocer carried the lumber home for me and stayed for a few hours to help me assemble it. I offered him more, but he shook his head, praised my dexterity with a hammer, and took home a signed copy of my book for his sister who wanted to be a dancer.

What carrying I did do finished off my knee. One day as I was climbing out of the bath tub, it jammed like a locked cog. It simply wouldn't straighten out. Sobbing from shock more than pain, I dried and dressed, hopped up the steps to the street, and took a taxi to the doctor. He sent me home with crutches and an appointment for surgery.

The procedure wasn't exactly botched, but I should have gone to a rehab center. Instead, given my lousy insurance, I headed straight back to vermin central. The neighbors — even the yellers — were helpful. Friends brought food and ran errands, as I battled to regain mobility.

I'd seen too many children dealing with disabilities to take this impairment very seriously. I told almost no one. But one very special person got word of my surgery – Winston, my Xhosa dancer. With some intervention from me but mainly due to his own amazing dynamism, he had made it to Boston, to my alma mater. He was ensconced there still, married to a lovely fellow Xhosa immigrant, and now a full professor, teaching African Studies. "Don't settle for good enough," he urged me on the phone, his warm baritone settling into my cochlear canal. "Remember what you kept telling me!"

We shared homesickness stories about South Africa and debated whether it would make sense for him and Lindi and their very American kids to go back, given all the changes taking place there.

And he asked me about Felix. He remembered us as a couple in Grahamstown, and I had told him about Felix's work. They had begun corresponding and still did, as far as I knew. I asked him not to tell my "true love," as he insisted on calling him. I was afraid of how much I was craving that contact. And how would I explain the whole breakup to Felix without making him feel somehow responsible?

Joanie and I take a break and I sink into a nap on the couch downstairs. I'm avoiding my bedroom, still feeling the pull of a dream last night. This is all it was: Instead of Felix's head on the pillow next to me, there was a large, red rose with a tangle of stamens at its center, like burnt electrical wires.

I still can't recall his death. I registered his silence, the deep peace next to me instead of the usual whiffling inhale and exhale, and turned on my bedside lamp, puzzled. What followed has disappeared behind a scrim, a barrier from which my brain recoils. The emergency service people swept in and did their thing. I must have called them. I know I went back to bed. Nothing else except reaching down to get one of his journals and the pang of pain in my hip. I remember nothing of the week that followed.

When I woke up this morning, I couldn't turn my head to look at his pillow, for fear of seeing that red rose.

The standoff with Joanie feels like a wound. Is that where that awful rose image has come from? What makes it worse is the sense that the wound is on her side, that this girl is hurting because of me, and I don't understand why.

ళ

The breakup with Charles involved a different kind of mental blackout, a willful escape into busyness. While searching for a new teaching position, I found a few part-time gigs – working behind the counter at a pastry store and as a receptionist at the hairdresser where I had my hair trimmed and babysitting for a family upstairs. On weekdays I walked their dog, Gunther, a sweet but high-strung German Shepherd that left swathes of fur on my pants. And I began working on my new book. Sales of *New Steps* were gradually increasing, and my editor was intrigued by the idea of a follow-up. Whenever I had a free morning, I planted myself either at my new Ikea desk (which I'd proudly assembled) or at one of the cafes in the neighborhood, armed with a notebook.

At first, all I did was make lists, idly pulling together topics I wanted to cover, and then winnowing them down in search of a clear, cohesive theme. Though far from gelling, the immersion in dance was like a benediction. My mind *jetéd* into that more desirable world. I had a mission, even if only a very vague one.

It wasn't until twenty months after the move to Brooklyn that I finally figured out how Charles uncovered my Los Angeles encounter with Felix.

~ 16 ~

Suspenders

I WAS A sucker. My husband had been cheating on me," I say to Joanie, my hands going idle, still clutching a handful of multicolored suspenders, some stretched out, others still usable. They used to make me smile, recalling Felix playing up this old-guy style. Charles would never have deigned to wear anything so inelegant. Joanie also stops what she's doing and listens, hands on hips.

"While he was getting angry with me about ancient history, he was in the middle of an affair of his own."

All these years later, I can still feel the humiliation. Hydra-like, it entangled me in tentacles of disbelief and indignation. I don't know which hurt more — that I had been thoroughly duped or that he'd found it so easy to sideline this pudgy, ungraceful spouse.

"Shit! Who with?"

"There'd probably been others, but this time it was a woman in his department."

"A coworker? Wasn't that a no-no?"

"Better than getting involved with a student. He did that two years earlier."

"How did you find out about this one?"

Thank goodness she is focusing on Charles and hasn't asked more about the man I had the fling with. How could I let on that when she was three, her father was betraying her mother with me? Not possible. On the other hand, telling her about Charles carries a certain satisfaction. He doesn't deserve to have his privacy protected and getting bitchy is bracing.

The more I recall his deceit, the harder I'm twisting the suspenders in my hands, until Joanie removes them and drops them into a garbage bag. I clutch at them for a moment. There are funny ones I bought him, with cartoon characters and biker logos and some in rainbow colors — but no one else is going to want them.

అ

So, there I was in the Brooklyn flat, with dinner guests just settling into their seats. On the mantelpiece, on either side of my little bronze Degas dancer I had arrayed Christmas and Hanukkah cards, and a vase of flowers from my publisher. The place was looking cozy, almost homey.

Life was looking up. The only hassle was the ongoing to-and-fro between Charles's team of lawyers and my one, an intrepid fellow who stopped charging me after a few months, but still refused to let me kowtow to their bullying. He reckoned I was being shafted out of much-needed income and that Charles should pay alimony, given how much higher his income was. Initially, I had refused to seek any money, but when he began quibbling over every possession – wanting all the records, claiming they were "a cohesive collection," and both Tiffany lamps, even though they'd been a gift to both of us, and even my tea pots, though he never much liked them – I agreed to fight back. So it was dragging on.

The phone rang as I was warming a sauce on the stove, adding some last-minute herbs. It was Dorothea, Charles's administrative assistant. She was a chatterbox, and we used to have some great gossip sessions but hadn't since the breakup. I greeted her warmly and wished her Merry Christmas. There was no return greeting.

"Another delay tactic from your damn lawyer! We're sick and tired of this shit," she squawked. "What do you think you're going to achieve? You're not getting him back, you know." I was stunned. Completely dumbfounded. "Are you there?" The squawk again. "Charles might be too much of a gentleman to say it, but you better cut out this greedy, grabbing crap, or we'll make sure you're left without a cent."

My guests had just arrived, a couple who lived on the top floor and a friend of theirs they'd been nagging me to meet. I simply put the phone down. I smiled brightly, made out it was a wrong number, just some crazy stranger.

But the implications of Dorothea's tirade registered in bursts all evening, in between eating and making conversation and trying to stay upright. That might have been Bunnington's finest performance. I kept hearing again the "we" and "You're not going to get him back." The late nights, that irritable distractedness, was that about work or Dorothea? I served the food and kept up my end of the conversation.

After they left, close to midnight, I called Charles. I let fly with the kind of fury only my mother and Felix ever heard from me, spiked with a huge added measure of pure hatred. All those months of guilt and humiliation had piled up like dry brush, and this was the match. My voice crackled. Oblivious of neighbors or passers-by who might overhear, I roared, "Charles Smith, you are a lying, cheating, morally repulsive hypocrite. I'm glad you found out about Felix. You fucking set me free."

He tried to hush me. Why? Because someone at his end might be disturbed? This was the fury he never got way back after that first fling with his student, and in a way he seemed to welcome it. He finally yelled back at me, things like "So what?" and "Don't get high and mighty with me." And then with his voice going deep and syrupy, he added, "You'd probably been cheating with that Felix of yours for years." He was goading me, enjoying my rage. I had a sick feeling that if we'd been face-to-face, he'd have reached out and tried to have sex, but I couldn't calm down.

"I wish I was screwing around," I bellowed, stomping around the apartment with the long phone cord snagging on the furniture. "Except for that one time, I've been faithful all these damn years while you've been fucking half your department. Just exactly when did this affair with Dorothea begin? And how many did you have before her?"

I didn't wait for a reply. Exhausted at last, I just pressed the button to disconnect and started untangling the cord. Then I washed the dishes. I showered, not worrying whether the water pipes disturbed the yellers next door. Eventually I tried to go to sleep, but the adrenalin — and coffee and chocolate cannoli — made that impossible. I picked up a book and put it down, turned on the TV but didn't watch it.

Lying wide awake on top of my bedspread, the question kept flashing: How did Charles find out about Felix? Had he been looking into my emails or recording my phone calls? But none of that would have told him what happened back in L.A.

It took me a few more sleepless nights and some quieter exchanges with Charles over the next few weeks to finally piece together his whole story. The more direct my questions got, the less he tried to shift the blame. And in the end, he denied nothing.

"You really pick winners, don't you?" my South African pal Angie said on the phone. Given that she knew all the preceding chapters, I owed her this part too. I called her one late January morning, after taking Gunther for a walk on the Brooklyn Heights promenade. The gray skyline of Manhattan and the persistent roar of traffic had sharpened my loneliness. "Can't say I ever trusted Charles. You were always making excuses for him, trying to see the best in him. At least with Felix you've always known exactly where you stand."

She was partly right. If Felix wasn't an open book, I've come to realize, he was never deceptive. Even the one unfamiliar woman I found on his cell phone has turned out to be a financial advisor ,seeking his business. She has called me too, but I've rebuffed her efforts to lure me in as a client.

I'm sorry about doubting you, my sweetheart. I wish so much he could hear that, though he'd have waved it aside.

Joanie and I stow some bags of garbage in the rubber bins outside and settle at the kitchen table. She puts out crackers and cheese, but I can't eat, not with this stuff welling to the fore. Joanie's still stewing over something, but she's looking me in the eye again, empathizing with my crazy story.

"Turns out," I say, "Charles's girlfriend had been trying to get pregnant, while pretending to be on birth control. Like in the old stories, classic-style hook-a-man technique."

"I didn't think anyone really did that. So he was trapped?"

"I didn't think girls did that either, but no, he wasn't actually trapped. More like they were playing each other. I gather he knew she was lying, and his attitude was if she got pregnant, he'd leave me and marry her, but not unless it happened. That much he admitted to me. He wasn't eager for upheaval, but he really wanted a kid."

"And you and he never… ?"

"Remember, I told you, I did get pregnant once, but I miscarried. It was after I'd been with that other man. I didn't know whose baby it was." Joanie's eyes go round. "It was terrible, not knowing. Charles assumed it had been his, and I let him think that. And I was never able to get pregnant again. It was almost like a punishment."

"No. Don't say that. Everyone makes mistakes." Joanie gives me a soft, sad look of pure sympathy, and then tilts her head, trying to puzzle out what's coming. "And his girlfriend did get pregnant?"

"No. She didn't, and she got suspicious. Finally, she confronted him. He declared love and devotion and agreed to go get tested — like he never did with me. Supposedly, he got tested during his first marriage and was assured everything was fine. I don't know if that was a mistake or deception by the doctor. Whatever, it turned out he'd been — as they say — shooting blanks all along. Totally sterile. And that's when it dawned on him that I must have been with someone else before my miscarriage."

Joanie forages in the fridge for something else to eat and then turns suddenly to face me, her eyes bulging. "You and Dad? That man you got pregnant with — that was Dad, wasn't it?" she whispers.

The blood is pounding in my ears. All I can think is *Sorry, Felix*. She stamps her foot in exaltation at her insight. "I thought so. Why didn't you tell me? I know you were lovers a long time ago, that you weren't always just buddies. Oh my God, you could have been my mother!"

I burst out laughing. What a glorious thought! But now there is no way not to come out with the whole story. I grab her arms then and draw her back onto her chair. Time for the truth.

"It was after you were born, my sweetheart. That's why I never said anything. It should never have happened, not when your mom and dad were already together, with a child. I'm so, so sorry. I didn't want you to think I was a home-wrecker. I didn't tell Felix until years later, and, of course, I wasn't sure it was his."

Joanie frowns and thinks.

185

I can almost hear the pieces clicking into place. And then she gives a deep shrug of her shoulders. "Mom and Dad were horrible together. They should have split up way earlier than they did. And you and Dad were stupid idiots. Why on earth did you waste so much time with other people?"

Good question. Free as a bird, now I can tell her just how huge the moment was when I realized for sure who my baby's father was. So many years after all that agonizing, finally it was clear. "It gave me so much pleasure and so much pain," I tell her.

In the heat of the moment I almost crowed about that to Charles, but some glimmer of the old protective urge silenced me. For all these years he'd so boldly asserted his masculinity, using the polio damage as a shield to ward off other fears, and now he'd discovered this other impairment. I knew how fiercely it had to sting. How could I not know? We'd been partners. I'd cared about him, loved him in the way one loves what you invest yourself in. And I'd striven to bolster his ego and make him happy for way too long to be able to switch off the awareness.

To his credit, Charles finally decided to play it bold, to make a fresh start. I say to Joanie, "He asked Dorothea to move in with him. And he suggested they find a sperm donor. It was a huge move for him. Maybe they were in love. I hope so, not for them but for their kid. She had artificial insemination and apparently got pregnant on the second or third try."

Having sympathy for Charles didn't stop me twisting the

knife just a little. I couldn't resist. In one of our cooler exchanges, I said to him, "You've told your mother about your relationship with Dorothea? I really miss talking with Ethel. Now that you've moved on with your life, you won't mind if she and I resume our friendship, would you?"

I tell Joanie about that, and she cackles. She's sitting with one leg folded under her and her elbows on the table, agog. "That must have made Chuck-the-Fuck flip out. Didn't you tell me once your husband said monogamy was the hallmark of the civilized man? And here you were, threatening to let his mama know just how uncivilized her wonderful son was."

"Exactly! I'd never have done it, but his reaction was very funny," I say. "I just wish I'd come up with that line before agreeing to move out of the apartment."

"You could have bribed him!" I high-five her, and she gets up and clears the table, dumping cups and plates any which way in the sink. Usually I cringe, waiting to hear something crack. Right now I'm too elated to worry.

I say, "Their kid must be in college by now." It hadn't dawned on me before.

"It was so unfair," Joanie exclaims. "Couldn't you have had a child that way? Or you could have adopted. Did he ever apologize? What a pig!"

She shakes her head, her lovely face all scrunched up in disgust, and then has to go pee. I'm left tying up more garbage bags, feeling pounds lighter. It's an odd feeling, caring more about this relationship than that marriage. I hear the water pipes, and it's as if the stale dregs of the break-up with Charles have finally been flushed away.

Felix saved me. I tell Joanie that fact over lunch the next day at a funky little café in St. James, the next community over. It has bright blue walls covered in paintings by local artists and fabulously weird chairs created by a township carpenter. We've walked all the way to Muizenberg and back and are ravenous. She orders the house salad and smoked snoek, being sensible, and then steals French fries from my burger platter. "They don't count if you don't order them for yourself," she says.

"Tell that to your twenty-pound baby," I say, but shovel most of them onto her plate. I'm hungrier than I've been in ages and I've ordered the "deluxe" version. There's plenty there to feed three.

She already knows some of my post-Charles story. "Dad didn't save you. You saved yourself," she says, the bold young feminist. "If you hadn't already done your first book and then gotten started on the second one and done all that wonderful teaching all over the world, you wouldn't have been able to move on."

I take a sitting bow. But Felix played a vital role. Over and over, just when I was feeling overwhelmed and thinking I should abandon my go-nowhere book project, the phone would ring, and there would be that energy-filled voice, ready to ignite another spark of excitement. I had friends and colleagues in the dance world who were helpful too, but nobody else could light up my mind like he did.

"By the way," she says, "what happened to the book? Weren't you doing it together?"

Ah yes, but that is another whole subject. Less worthy of a bow, and pushed out of my mind till recently.

That second book began to evolve in a different direction, one that might have offered a glorious new chapter in our lives. Instead, we — Felix and I — let it slip away. I failed him. And, let's face it, he failed me too. He also gave up on it, despite all his early enthusiasm.

They say you shouldn't expect other people to complete you, but that is what couples aspire to. We did in some ways — eventually, but not in others, I suppose.

~ *17* ~

Files

Over the next sixteen years, between that first meeting with the kids and when I came to live with Felix, we met up five times. Three were with Joanie and Trevor, one of those with gorgeous, exuberant Nellie, and two just him and me. Strange to reduce those years to this math, but right now I'm stock-taking.

With the kids, the connection just got better through the years as we became correspondents, exchanging phone calls and birthday cards, and then emails. I became their long-distance, go-to adult, helping them out with material for school projects, and they'd return the favor with snippets of youth culture they thought I'd enjoy.

Professionally, I was doing well, traveling widely, teaching teachers and doing workshops with children, writing articles and research papers, and it gave me a kick to incorporate what I learned from Felix's kids.

With their dad it was more complicated. Though after my initial post-Charles shut-down, we communicated quite often, I didn't tell him the entire divorce story until long after I learned the facts, and that frustrated him. "You keep me in the dark in more ways than one," Felix complained, "and not the kind I'd like to be in with you."

He didn't know how much it pleased me that he still wanted to bridge that gap. I didn't let on either my suspicion that if I wasn't elusive, his interest would wane, complicated by guilt – his and mine. So long as I kept my distance, he was safe playing the ardent admirer. He knew, of course, that Charles and I had split up, but I'd let him think we'd just drifted apart. I couldn't bring myself to spell out his part in our rupture.

Then, in the summer of 2003 he was in town for business discussions about one of his therapy devices, and we arranged to meet at the model boat pond in Central Park, that setting of a million romantic movie scenes. There was something more open about him, more emotional. He had been asking about my life and my friends and whether I was involved with anyone. I started to talk about trust and the next thing I knew the Charles saga erupted from its tightly sealed cavity.

There was a long silence when I finished speaking. "I'm glad you broke free of him," Felix said. He hugged me. "What an asshole, a user. You always made him sound like such a decent man, but shit – that wasn't decent. It was disgusting.

And I'm sorry I wasn't there for you when you needed support."

He looked down, cradling my hand between his. "And I'm so, so sorry. You're the last person I'd ever want to hurt. You know that, don't you? If I'd only known; I wish you'd told me. But why do you always take so long to tell me about these things?"

We rose and walked the circumference of the pond and finally settled again on a bench, watching the miniature yachts scudding across the water. Felix looked around at me then, the tiger eyes with their frame of fine lines still a color like no one else's – except his son's. "This is fucked up," he said. "You're free now, but I'm not. I'm actually being honorably monogamous these days. Aren't you impressed? Nellie and I are in counseling, doing all the stuff I never believed in, really trying."

He brought my hand to his lips. "However, Copper Girl, that doesn't mean I'm immune to you. My heart still hammers when I see you walking towards me."

Would he have said that at an earlier time? Probably not. Even with sex off the table, or perhaps even more so because of that, we seemed acutely attuned to one another. Repeatedly, we started speaking about the same topic at the same moment. "Snap!" I said, and we burst out laughing.

For the first time, he was the one speculating about relationships and what draws people together. "It's so strange and so intertwined with the past," he said. I listened with delight and confusion.

"Like our past?" I asked.

"You think it colors how we respond to new people?"

"The deep past, childhood," he said. "Maybe it's what made you so trusting with Charles. Think how your father treated you, and how your mother made you feel. As for my mother, our therapist says I try to win over every woman I meet, to rewrite that history. I don't know."

It was harder than ever to part. He walked me to the downtown subway entrance before taking an uptown train himself, and we stood there talking for another ten minutes, and then another and another. He was wearing his leather jacket with the patches, and as I finally walked away, he reached into the inside pocket and I heard notes from a harmonica.

By the time we met up again a few years later, the landscape was altered. Nellie had found herself a young stud and told Felix she was moving on. I heard about all that in a long, long phone call. My heart did a little hop – a *what-if* that I tried to suppress. It was way too soon.

For all I know he precipitated the break-up. Maybe not. Either way, he voiced no criticism of her. And again, he insisted that they stay close, this time for Trevor's sake. "He's very adolescent," Felix said, "and pretty wild. He needs me around, or God alone knows what he'll get up to."

He wasn't about to admit it, but I think he was bruised. Being dumped isn't fun, especially when you're being replaced by someone younger. I could vouch for that. Come to think of it, being jettisoned when there's no one else in the picture might be even worse .

I'd done that myself to a couple of men along the way.

But this guy still twisted my heart. Felix sounded lost, and not just on the domestic front. Work wasn't the source of satisfaction it had always been. He had a new boss, hired over his head from another university, a play-it-safe kind of guy obsessed with budgets and inhospitable to out-of-the-box innovations. I'd never heard Felix so dispirited. And that's when this huge notion bloomed in my brain.

I said, "How about we collaborate on my book? What if we bring our two fields together? I've got all these lovely stories of how dance connects kids and opens their horizons, but there is another whole aspect I haven't touched, that I wouldn't know how to handle. I'm really stuck. Could you tell me about techniques that help disabled children move more freely — so they can also express themselves through music?"

Felix was quiet for a beat or two, and then he said something I didn't catch. I said, "What?" and he boomed back, "I'd love that. I don't know what would fit with your vision — you'd have to guide me — but I could show you a dozen different avenues to explore. The new research on mobility is amazing — especially the stuff dealing with young bodies." That was more like the Felix I knew.

I suggested we meet for a weekend somewhere and work out an outline. He positively purred, "Mmm, yes!" I laughed. That felt so good.

The phone calls and emails flew. It took us weeks to clear our calendars and settle on a date, and then we couldn't agree on a location. I suggested we meet at the top of the Empire State Building.

He emailed back that perhaps we should try Casablanca.

"Bogart and Bergman can't hold a candle to us," he wrote.

We thought we were very funny. Turned out we were chicken, seriously scared. And aside from anything else, in our phone conversations the book had begun to take shape and neither of us wanted to risk ruining that.

"What if we fight, who gets custody of the outline?" I asked.

"And given our track record, we're likely to fight," he said.

"Let's play it by ear," I suggested.

Eventually, we settled on a picturesque-looking bed-and-breakfast place in Greenport, a few hours out of New York City, on Long Island. I called and booked two rooms, being sensible. Trying to be sensible – and not to think too far ahead. It was enough to face just the possibilities of this weekend.

As the date drew nearer, I started to get antsy. Aside from a few very forgettable link-ups, usually when I was traveling, it was a while since I'd had close contact with a man. It felt even longer since I'd felt a truly tender touch. Affectionate hugs, yes, with friends and my students, but no real touching.

And Felix hadn't seen my torso in a very long time. I began doing sit-ups. A week before, I noticed how papery my skin was becoming and began applying an almond-extract lotion. On impulse I splurged on a pedicure. My feet were still knobbly, ugly from all the years of abuse, but I came home with smoother heels and pink toenails. I even considered dying my hair, making it as auburn as it used to be, but that felt too risky. What if it came out scarlet? At the last minute, from the depths of my cosmetic drawer I retrieved an almost empty bottle of Chanel and slipped that into my overnight bag.

Prompt as always, at ten on the Saturday morning, I arrived at the gray and blue Victorian B&B. The owner was serving morning tea in the foyer and came forward to welcome me, looking about expectantly for my companion. The place was even prettier than the picture I'd spotted on the Internet, but there was no sign of Felix. With my cases stowed in my room, hair brushed, and lipstick refreshed, I went back downstairs to wait. An hour past our agreed meeting time, the tea things had been cleared and I'd finished reading the publicity literature and was beginning to seethe. *Typical! Probably sightseeing his way along the local road, getting into conversations at every farm stand.*

Half an hour later, in strode Dr. Barnard, brisk as ever, his gray hair pulled back in a snazzy pony tail. He dropped his shoulder bag at my feet and said, "Reporting for duty, you lovely woman. Ready for action." My anger evaporated and the nervousness flooded back.

I told him where his room was. He gave me a strange look but said nothing, just trotted off to deposit his belongings. We ate lunch at a harbor-front café and went for a walk, exploring antique stores and art galleries, and then worked all afternoon on the big, shady verandah, exchanging lists of topics we'd each made about people and places we wanted to feature. Concentration didn't come easily, but I thought we were productive. In the evening we went to a glorious outdoor ballet performance. The stage was in an orchard, and each time the music subsided, the air filled with a twittering backdrop of insect song.

Just sitting next to him in the moonlight was making me happy, shoulders and thighs touching, until the ground got too hard and we accepted an offer of two folding chairs from the family next to us. Felix became very quiet, evidently absorbed in the spectacle. I knew the piece and liked this dance company, but what I wanted was to be lying in his arms — on that grass or in a bed, naked.

On the way back to our B&B, Felix pulled into the shadowy parking lot of a boarded-up frozen yogurt joint. I was puzzled. After all, we had not one but two beds waiting for us back at the house. On the other hand, it was fun to play at being teenagers, grabbing a chance like this to neck where we might be interrupted by the cops.

I undid my seatbelt with pulse fluttering and turned to him, my hand on his thigh and expecting him to be reaching for me. My breasts were tingling in anticipation of his touch. But he was sitting facing forward, with his seatbelt still buckled.

He said, "You booked separate rooms."

"To be discreet, to give us sleeping options — not for any other reason."

He was silent, his chin tucked down on his chest. To lighten the mood, I added, "I snore these days, you know. Didn't want to keep you awake."

"You always snored," he said. "I didn't mind then and I wouldn't mind now. You know how soundly I sleep — or you used to know."

My heart started thudding. How could such a seemingly practical decision have caused this withdrawal? After all the delicious anticipation…

"I want to sleep with you," I muttered. It was the bluntest I'd ever been in my life.

"I know," he whispered, and for a moment I got indignant. Had I been that obvious? "I want to sleep with you too, my Copper Girl. Every time we get together, the chemistry's incredible — as hot as ever. But when I saw you'd booked separate rooms it started me thinking. This is crazy, but I don't think we should make love."

"You're saying you're not interested anymore?" In the white zigzag of street light, I could see him taking deep breaths. It didn't make sense.

"No," he groaned and squeezed my hand. "That would make this easier. You know what you do to me. But I also know what I do to you emotionally — or what I might do to you. I've learned a lot about pain this past year, Sal, how people can hurt each other, even without meaning to.

"We've got these two days together and then what? Would you be okay with this, with us making love like two crazy kids, and then just moving on? Who knows when we'll see each other again, who we'll come across in between. I don't want to hurt you again. I treasure our connection. I don't want to risk losing it."

I yanked my hand away. I wanted to slap him or shout the way I did that very first time we tried to have sex at Rhodes.

I did hiss, "After all these damn years, when the coast is clear, and when it would be just fine with me, now you've got scruples? Now you don't want to make love to me?"

He sat there in silence, clutching my hand, not letting me withdraw it. Bugs from the swarm circling the street light bashed against the window. I wanted to squash them.

But Felix was right. It was too soon for him. And at the back of my mind, even as my excitement grew about the weekend, I'd been bracing for the pain of separating afterwards. Neither of us was about to uproot and move across the country, not immediately. Would he go back to San Francisco and be faithful until we could meet again? That wasn't likely. He was single again and surely going to play the field. And I would have gotten angry. Sex does change things.

Finally, I reached over and ran my fingers over his ear and down his sinewy neck, hooking them into his hair. For a moment I leaned forward, wanting to kiss the down-turned corner of his mouth, pretty sure that if I did, he would turn and kiss me back, and we would burst past his hesitation.

Instead I withdrew my fingers and sat back. "Oh, fuck it. I never thought I'd say this, but you're growing wise in your old age, Felix Barnard."

At my room door he kissed me briefly. He looked into my eyes and his hands lingered on my cheeks and then fell away. I stood there, watching him walk down the passage to his room, still with those cowboy bowed legs. He turned and shout-whispered, "Breakfast at eight? Sleep well, Copper Girl."

It was a long, uncomfortable night. When we met in the dining room the next morning, he cast me a silent, inquiring stare, an "Are you okay?" I shrugged and went about loading my plate with scrambled eggs and kippers from the big silver serving dishes. Our hostess fussed around us, offering coffee and fresh toast and her homemade preserves, and we chatted with her as if everything was just fine.

We put in a few hours of work, sitting on the beach with shirts on over our swimsuits, our papers weighed down with a suntan lotion bottle and shoes. Felix had come with case studies, neatly typed and grouped in manila folders, and some brief outlines of theories he thought could be interwoven with my stories of dance sessions in various places. There was trouble though. He was running into territorial blocks put up by one of the other researchers, who wasn't happy about their work featuring in a book aimed at a non-academic audience.

There was some territoriality between us, too. What had seemed so clear when we first discussed the collaboration wasn't as clear now that we were getting to specifics. I wanted it to focus on the children as social, interactive beings, and Felix – for all his concern for their wellbeing – felt the crux of our contribution lay in the physical possibilities.

He said, "I don't think you understand what I'm trying to say. Let me explain."

"Don't condescend to me," I snapped back, digging my toes into the sand. "I fully understand – but you're not hearing me. In case you've forgotten, I've been working in this field a long time." We went back to our lists, but what had been collaborative now felt like jousting. Around us, families called and laughed and radios blared. Everyone else was having fun. We were not.

After a while he suggested we go for a swim. We slipped off our shirts, put our respective folders into our respective bags, and set off across the sand. The waves were swelling high and rough, and hardly anyone else was in the water. A few times they pushed us together and we rocked with the current, chest to chest, before separating. It pleased me that I was slimmer than last time he'd seen me, and my black swimsuit dipped low in front. He looked pretty good himself, heavier around the middle but brown as ever, with white curls down the groove of his chest.

We'd been drinking a lot of water on the beach, slaking thirst from the kippers at breakfast. My bladder was full. The bouncing wasn't helping. When he said, "I need to pee," that did me in. I told him I had to also and moved towards the shore. "So, do it," he said. "No one can see and the salt water rinses you clean." All my conditioning went against such a thing; I could hear Imma's disapproval, but the need was great. I took a few moments to relax enough and finally release a hot gush into the surrounding cold. Sweet relief. I felt liberated and light.

Felix was staring at the horizon, clearly not as comfortable.

"I thought you had to pee too," I said.

"I did, but we don't work like you women. You're making it hard for me, so to speak." And he grinned.

"Think about taxes," I said.

Just then a wave knocked us apart. I tumbled under the froth and when I came back up, spluttering and blinking, a family with shrieking kids had swept up close and Felix was yards away, laughing as he tried to plow his way back against the undertow.

Eventually, we dried off and went to have dinner at a fish-

and-chips joint overlooking the sunset water. We talked about what Joanie and Trevor were up to, and politics, and music. We didn't mention the book or us. Back at the house, again we kissed goodnight at my door and for a moment I held his face between my hands as he'd held mine the night before, and then let go.

Checking out the next morning Felix nearly lost his cool. Our hostess, evidently, had watched us book in with suspicion, and ended up delighted with us. "If you'll forgive me saying this, I wish the young people of today could be like the two of you," she said, fingers caressing the crucifix on her chest. She looked up coyly. "My husband would tell me to mind my own business, but anyone with half an eye could tell the two of you are in love. You are, aren't you? If you do marry, your union will be all the more blessed because you've stayed chaste."

We glanced quickly at each other and I could see written all over Felix's rueful dial the memory of how unchaste we'd been way, way back. I felt my face flush as I thanked her, picked up my bag, and headed for the exit.

"Blessed, my fucking foot," Felix snorted, catching up with me. "She should only know how hard this has been." He looked ready to turn and go back to the desk. I linked my arm through his and drew him out the door.

"*If you do marry...*"

As we waved goodbye and started our cars, I wondered when I'd ever see him again, or if. We still had the book, maybe. Our precious project, our reason for coming together this weekend, felt as faded as the umbrellas on the beach, a thing of the past. But perhaps it could be resuscitated.

I tried to hold onto that thought as I wove back into ghastly stop-start traffic, struggling to keep at bay a lurking sense of loss. A tide was ebbing from my life. *If we ever got married...* I was yielding a hope, a faint notion of possibility I didn't even know I'd been clutching so fervently through all these years.

~ *18* ~

Book Covers

O n Eric's third day, he and I go on a "date." Joanie insists. She wants time to herself to photograph and rest, "and commune with my dad."

Eric is eager to pick up some books on South African architecture and innovations in the use of low-cost solar technology and recycled materials. We explore three stores, an amazingly quaint one around the corner from us in Kalk Bay, and two in suburban malls. We take a break for lunch at a hotel with a view of the mountain, a white wedding cake of colonial splendor utterly devoid of solar anything except the shade of huge, ancient oak trees. We take guilty pleasure in the lush lawns and speculate if they're using recycled water, given the growing shortage in the city. In his measured way, Eric fills me in on the latest nonsense from the election campaign back home – his home, not mine, though I forget that sometimes. It feels good. I haven't thought about anything outside my own four walls in so long.

Then we hit the two best bookstores in the city center. I'm starting to fade in the last one when I hear, "Ms. Paddington?" The manager, a wiry fellow with feet turned out and a face that is all elevated profile, is holding a copy of *New Steps*, the back cover, with its portrait of me, facing up.

"Yup, guilty as charged," I say. It's impressive that he's recognized me. The photo is a studio shot, with my hair still quite dark, drawn smoothly back, ballet-style. The focus is very soft and flattering. In front of him is the reality, this makeup-less almost 70-year-old, with white hair spiraling in every direction, in a flowing mumu. Eric stands at my side with his shopping bags, amused, watching to see what happens next.

"I used to be a dancer and I'm a huge fan. Will you autograph this? And a few more copies?" The man's eyes have gone rounder. He evidently feels brazen, taking a chance like this. "We could do a wonderful promotional event and perhaps offer these as prizes."

Eric speaks up: "If you think there would be that much interest, how about raffling them, and donating the funds to a dance troupe in the townships?" I give him a "You go, boy!" nudge with my elbow. The manager is even more excited now. I guess what's coming next and it does: He asks if I will come to speak at the store. Then he mentions he heard a while back that there was a second book in the works.

"Yes." I feel very odd, admitting to that embryonic entity. "It was called *Next Steps*, but we never finished it."

"Ah, that *is* a shame. Do you think you ever might finish writing it?" he asks.

Eric turns to me, eyebrows raised in curiosity. I'm not sure what to say next. After I came to live with Felix, we talked about picking up the book, but we were too busy being retired. About six months ago, Felix got a bee in his bonnet again because of a big-name conference organized by his old department at Stanford University. He kept bringing up new angles or approaches we could try. The participants were going to be exploring the overlap between high-tech therapeutic techniques and the psychological boost provided by recreational approaches. He was asked to participate but had to decline on his neurologist's advice, reluctantly.

"If it wasn't for the flying... We should have done the presentation together," he said. "We have something to contribute, you and I. And we should get that book out there." But then we both went back to puttering. Were we scared to rock this gently bobbing boat? I remembered how we locked horns that weekend on Long Island; I have no idea if he did. Neither of us mentioned it.

The bookstore manager's forehead wrinkles into up-pointing arrows in consternation. He whispers, "Oh, I'm so sorry, I forgot. I heard that you lost your — er — your partner. May I offer my condolences?" I thank him, and promise I'll call to arrange a date in a while, after the memorial, and once the house is sold. *If I'm still around.*

Thank goodness for *New Steps.* Not that sales have been

all that lucrative – though for a book of its kind, it has done remarkably well for a long time – but it did boost my reputation in the field. That led to consultation gigs, and guest lectureships, and some fabulous trips to dance centers on every continent. A second book would have been an extension of that, with so many other aspects to explore. The failure irks me on various levels and thinking about it puts me in a bad mood.

⤚ٸ

Heading home to Kalk Bay, with him at the wheel this time, Eric says, "You mentioned selling the house. Do you really want to do that?"

Another rough subject. I feel less constrained with him than with Joanie. For all the sharing she and I have done, the house stuff still feels like landmine terrain. I've steered clear of it and so has she. To Eric I say, "No. I don't know where the hell I'm going to go."

He's driving faster than I would but he's competent. Fortunately, he's keeping his eyes on the road and won't notice my glum expression. Tears start to rise. This is ridiculous. I haven't cried in all these months, and now I'm going to cry about the house? I swallow hard and say, "But it needs to be sold so you can get the money and split it with Trevor. If I could buy it from the estate I would, but I don't have near enough in the bank. But promise me – seriously, you have to promise you won't say anything about this to Joanie."

"No, I won't promise that," he says and does cast a quick glance at me. "Joanie thinks you want to get away, that you're eager to make a fresh start somewhere else, away from sad

207

memories, and she's hurt by that. Why on earth didn't you tell her how you feel? Now she just wants to get rid of it as soon as possible — and you know what she's like once she gets an idea in her head."

I shrug. "I couldn't bear for her to feel sorry for me, or obligated. I suppose I'm just not good at saying what's on my mind."

He downshifts like a race car driver and swoops through a curve. "Look, it's not up to me, but maybe we can make a plan. I would love to be able to come back here year after year with our kids."

So I take the leap, as if I've shifted gears too. "I could rent it from you." Now I'm looking sideways at him. "The money wouldn't be anywhere near what you could get if you sell or if you rent it out as a holiday home — so it's cheeky for me to suggest it — but it would be year-round. And obviously you could stay any time you want, the more often the better."

"Hmm, perhaps. Let's see what Joanie and Trevor think," Eric says. I can see he's weighing ideas of his own. "I hear you're pretty good with tools. If there was some way we could keep the house, would you be interested in working with me the next time we come, perhaps on a second bathroom and another bedroom?"

He parks in the driveway and gets out with all his packages. Before we head inside, he gives me a kiss on my forehead. "I'll speak to the wife."

A while later, the lovers go out for a walk. There's a strange silence in the house that wasn't there before they filled it with their energy. I'm happy to have some quiet time, and a chance to tidy up. The place looks like a hurricane has come through, books and papers everywhere, clothes lying about, glasses and plates. *She's Felix's kid*, I think. As South Africans would say, she makes a *gemors* wherever she goes. People like them don't fuss over minor stuff.

With order at least partially restored in the living room, I do one more constructive thing – or take the first step: I drag out from under my bed the second box, the one with a layer of dust covering two neat stacks of manila folders. Files from Stanford? Or the prosthetic company Felix worked with in San Francisco? I sit on the rug with the box between my legs.

There are headings scrawled on each file, and as I lift one and then another and another, I see *"Sally's chapter suggestions."* They are the pages I sent Felix months after our working weekend in Greenport. And there is *"Iceland, Ireland, Israel,"* a collection of mini-essays on what I saw and loved in those countries, and paper-clipped to each one are pages of typed and handwritten notes.

Recognition dawns. For stunned minutes I sit, hands resting palm up on the floor, aghast that we let so much go to waste. Neither of us called it quits on the book; we just got sidetracked by competing priorities. I was conducting my workshops and doing speaking engagements and travelling. He'd been involved with the restructuring of his department and training new staff members. Every now and then one of us would suggest we meet and push forward, but then we'd get bogged down with more pressing matters.

Finally, in an email, I told him I was putting the book on ice for now and would let him know when I was ready again to give it real attention. He simply said, "As you wish. I understand." He never let on how much work he'd already done, gathering all kinds of data and background.

Around that time, I got involved with a charming Argentinian orchestra conductor five years my junior. After a while, he began staying with me when he had concerts in New York, and every few months he'd send me a ticket to some exotic locale, insisting it was the most romantic spot in the world. We had fun and I was proud of myself for moving on. For a long time after the heartbreaking stay in Greenport, the thought of connecting with any man had made my skin crawl. It took courage to open up again.

If I thought about Felix, a terrible gap loomed where our friendship had been, but I did my best not to think much about him and what might have been. It must have been at least two years since we'd actually spoken. Instead, we exchanged articles or jokes, and now and then he sent me links to his favorite new phenomenon, flash mobs of dancers and singers. He challenged me to see if I could organize one on the promenade overlooking the East River. I did it – with the help of a bunch of students from the Brooklyn Academy of Music. It was hilarious. I sent him a video of the event taped by a colleague and got back a texted cheer, all in caps like an old telegram: "CONGRATULATIONS! WISH I'D BEEN THERE. KNEW YOU COULD DO IT."

Felix began talking about retiring and going back to South Africa. The next thing I knew, it was a *fait accompli*. I was shocked that it happened so quickly, and unexpectedly sad that he was that much farther away. I guessed he might have hooked up with another woman, that maybe that's why I hadn't heard much from him. And for all I knew, given the trouble with Charles, he was keeping his distance so as not to cause problems with my conductor boyfriend. When Guillermo broke up with me, having gotten engaged to a violinist from Cologne, I didn't bother mentioning it to Felix until months later.

❦

I get up, stretch and bend, and I'm about to shove the box back under the bed when I stop myself. No, this treasure trove doesn't go back into the shadows. It belongs out in the open, where I can get to grips with what he's written. The material might be indecipherable, or maybe not. It could be out of date, or not. A seedling of curiosity starts poking through the lethargic layers of my brain. What would Felix have suggested for that dewy-eyed child in Ethiopia with a leg withered from a birth injury? What would help the little girl in Wisconsin with cerebral palsy, or those bombing victims in Iraq? Could we help bring some rhythm and joy into lives that have been so limited? I can't wait to see what he wrote, once I have time to myself again.

Odd notion, but I want it up in the attic – that space we've been so diligently emptying. Maybe on Felix's table. I can't get the box up there, but Eric could. I'll ask him later.

Finally, I put that all aside and collapse on my bed with a mug of hot chai tea. I have the last journal: "#5, 1967, Brazil." There's that smudged, added-on phrase, and this time I can make out the words, "*plus PE/Grhmtn*" on the spine. Flicking through the pages, I spot mentions of the carnival in Rio, and the Amazon, and Argentina, where he talked with a famous orthopedic surgeon, a friend of John Latimer's.

> *Maria has to meet this man. He is brilliant. They let me watch from the gallery as he and his team worked on a guy who got crushed in a building collapse. We talked for hours afterwards, with his terrible English and my worse Portuguese, and he showed me before and after photos of some of his other cases. If anyone could do something about her legs it's this guy.*

Ah, and the two parts crash together like cymbals. If Maria was disabled, how was she his flamenco teacher? I dig under the bed for the journals and pull out the Spain volume. This time around I read his talk of the amazing Maria and register for the first time that her friend was demonstrating the steps, not her. Tossing out one journal and then another, I go looking for clues. Other questions pop up, about the time they spent in Switzerland years later, when he was working on different approaches to muscle regeneration. I remember photos of the lovely, smiling woman, never shown full-length.

With my brain more awake than in months, I promise myself I will ask Maria herself, but their story is becoming clear: Felix took a shine to his flamenco teacher. Perhaps they were lovers at the start but not for long. What mattered more was his desperate desire to help her. Why this boy from Port Elizabeth had such a drive I don't know, but his whole career seemed to find its direction from her. And she did everything in her power to encourage and support him, not just for her own sake, but for his. That's why she was a real friend — even though he never did manage to restore her mobility.

Lying diagonally across the bed, with Felix's pillow squished under my cheek, my mind riffles back to my own exchange with Maria. She might not have been able to walk, but she certainly put things in motion. It was she who asked me to come when Felix had his first aneurism – and now finally I understand why.

Out of the blue, I had received an email from her. Puzzled by the unfamiliar "from" name, I glanced at the message on my cell phone, thinking it might be a sales pitch, and then realized with a gasp who this was.

"Sally, I am a friend of Felix Barnard. He is very ill and he wishes to see you. Please call me." There was a number with a 34-93 area code.

The world around me vanished. Nauseous with fear, barely able to see, I found a quiet corner and dialed immediately, my fingers trembling. I got the numbers twisted and had to click off and start again. The third time I got it right. The dring-dring-dring underscored the prayer running through my head, "Please, Felix, don't die. Please, Felix, hold on. Please, Felix."

Maria had assumed I was in New York. In fact, I was in Africa, attending a United Nations cultural conference in Nairobi. In the evenings, we talked on panels, facing tiers of adults. During the day, we had groups of children coming to learn dances from around the world. It had been an exciting, absorbing week, but all through it, at the back of my mind, I'd held onto the idea that when it was over, before heading back to New York, just maybe I would extend my trip and head south. I wanted to go see friends in South Africa – and perhaps visit Felix, if I could track him down.

Now he might not be there to visit. I might never see him again, never touch him again.

Maria, on the phone from Barcelona, told me about the cottage in Kalk Bay and the two neighbors who saw Felix collapse in his yard. They found her number in his wallet and guessed she must be a close friend.

"I called him at the hospital now, this morning," she said. "He kept asking me to find you, to tell you. I know who you are; you are this Sally he has loved all these years. My husband, he looked for you on the Internet. He got your email address from your publisher."

I registered "husband" with faint surprise, and then that she was saying, "I would go to Felix myself, but I am not able to help him, to look after him. And anyway, he is asking for you. Please, Sally, please can you go?"

"I can be in Cape Town by tomorrow night," I said. My whole life had just flipped over, all its shapes and clear priorities turned upside down. "Which hospital is he in?"

~ *19* ~

Invitations

I'm back at work on the house, keeping myself busy and trying not to think about my own stupidity, and not obsess about the future. I don't know if Eric has spoken to Joanie, or if she has called Trevor. Given that they've said nothing, I'm assuming the answer is no to my renting. Heartsore, but I want everything shipshape so they get the best possible sale price.

Up in the attic, I pull out the calendars for Joanie to discard or keep. It's not an urgent task, but more and more I'm choosing to spend time up here. The vast expanse of blues — of sea and sky and distant mountains — eases my mind. I have no special plan for the calendars, but on top is the purple-crested one from 1970, with the missing page – November – the month before Felix and I parted in Grahamstown.

I have that in my hand when the doorbell rings. I clamber down the rickety stairs and find the minister at the door. He wants to talk to me about the memorial.

"Forgive me for coming by like this without calling first," he says. "You mentioned that when Dr. Barnard's daughter was here you'd make a decision. I don't want to be a nuisance, but my dance card is getting rather full, and I want to make sure I can fit it in while she's here."

Without asking if he wants tea, I excuse myself and go to put on a kettle, because that's how people do things here, and it gives me a chance to ponder my response. Perhaps he would like his "usual" but it's too early for alcohol. As the water begins to rumble, I call out to him, "We do have a plan taking shape, just not quite finalized."

I hear an "Aha" and leave that hanging while I put together the cups and saucers and empty a packet of rather bland Marie biscuits into a bowl. Joanie probably bought them to stop her nausea. I bring the tray back into the living room and set it down on the table between us.

As I'm about to pour the tea I say, "I appreciate your kindness very much, and I do hope you'll attend, but we won't be needing your professional services." That hasn't been discussed, but I'm quite clear about it. If Joanie has other ideas – tough, but I'm pretty sure she doesn't. Felix is not going to get squeezed into a prayerfulness he never valued and certainly never taught to his children.

Rev. Halibut – is that his real name, or was it just the fishy stare that makes me think that? — stammers, and then says with careful cordiality, "Ah well then, goodness me, I wouldn't want to force myself on you. But what exactly do you have in mind?"

Rage is rising, building from a spark to a flame.

Hypocritical old sod! He damn well would want to force himself, to make us do things the way he thinks is right. We're godless heathens as far as he's concerned, and he wants to save us from ourselves.

For so long I've been polite around such moralistic types, but I'm not inclined to be that way anymore. As I'm about to let fly, to tell him what I think, my eye falls on the Rhodes calendar I brought downstairs. I hold up my hand to indicate he should wait, be silent, give me a moment.

My gut-brain has thrust up the memory of the pain that erupted as I read Felix's note that ghastly evening. I taste again the urge to rave and yell and shriek in the empty apartment. I want to do it again now to this poor, mild-mannered man. *This time your wonderful friend Felix, that shit, didn't even leave me a note.*

And then, sitting there holding the brown tea pot, my hands go heavy and movement ceases. I'm immobilized within a restraining bubble of silence. I feel Felix, almost see him — not old Felix or young Felix, just the essence of tiger-Felix — wrapping me in an embrace of fierce tenderness. I hear "No, Sal, you know it wasn't like that…" The sensation lasts a few seconds and fades. Steam rising from the tea fills my nose with sweet fragrance, and as I pour the color deepens into a glorious red-gold.

"You and Felix had an extraordinary partnership," the

minister says. "He didn't tell me much, but it was abundantly clear. With you around, he became contented, at peace. The change was quite astounding, but of course you know that." Halibut – oh no, not Halibut, Halpert – continues, "He cared for you so very deeply. Have never felt that way myself. I envied him."

I look at him and all the anger has evaporated.

Could Felix have been afraid that I would leave him? That thought has never entered my head before. It makes me choke. I take a gulp of hot tea and swallow hard to open my throat. Felix didn't leave Deidre, or Nellie either. He didn't even choose to leave his mother; she pushed him out. While I was so wrapped up in my own insecurity, perhaps that guy, so devil-may-care, so buoyant, was contending with a deep dread of loss of his own. Who knows how long it took him to overcome it – if he ever did?

The minister is watching me, eyes kind and concerned, not rushing things. My voice is hoarse but as calmly as he spoke to me, I say to him, "You are a good man, a good shepherd for your flock. I would really like you to be part of our little farewell event, to speak about your friendship with Felix and to sing with us. There will be some great music, if you don't mind hanging out for an hour or two with a raggle-taggle pack of wolves like us."

His shoulders go down. I hadn't realized till now that they were hunched up. He grins like an adolescent who's been invited to the cool party and says, "Let me know when and where. I'll be happy to take part. I've got more wolf in me than you might suspect."

We'll see how the event goes, but I have a feeling I've inherited a friendship, and it will be very welcome. I might even start drinking whisky.

❧

That night when I walked into Felix's hospital room and saw him hooked up to monitors, eyes closed, I knew I'd come home. There was nowhere else in the whole wide world that I wanted to be more than in that buzzing, neon-lit room, next to this snoring, sunken-cheeked man.

The nurse left us alone and I whispered his name. No response. I said it again. His eyelids flickered and half-opened. His gaze found me, focused, and brightened just a glimmer. The corner of his lips curled. A hand reached out from under the blanket, and I grabbed it in both of mine and kissed it. "Please hang in. Don't give up, please – for me."

"Copper Girl." His voice was raspy. "You're here. I'll stay if you'll stay." I believed him.

"I'm not leaving," I said.

❧

So here I was, in Kalk Bay, with no more clothing than I'd brought with me to the conference in Kenya. I'd blown off the return half of my ticket back to New York, had Sherrie rent out my little basement flat, and Felix-and-Sally were finally a couple. Not married. Why on earth bother with ceremonies and licenses? But very much a couple.

Felix's recovery was slow but it gave us time to adapt to one another and gradually build a rhythm of co-existence. His messy, ramshackle house took some adjusting to too, though I loved it right away, even with its rust and peeling paint and the eccentric marine decor. There were tasks to do that Felix hadn't bothered with, but once I started he was quite happy to get on board. Scraping and sanding and repairing gave me a sense of belonging and helped him regain strength. There is still masses to do, but we accomplished a fair amount.

We cooked together, shopped together, worked together in the garden, planting and pruning, most of the time without clashing over anything. Though we didn't have sex – both too scared to raise his blood pressure? – there was much cuddling and constant caressing. We slept spooned together, first one on the inside curve, then the other, turning over to ease a sore joint but never out of touch. Aside from arguments about his care, me nagging him to take things easy and him trying to forget the whole aneurism thing, shared habitation came surprisingly easily. My tiger guy wasn't tamed but he had made peace with himself. Prissy Bunnington had mellowed too.

But I was curious. We'd agreed not to waste time looking back, but eventually I had to ask: "You took long enough, but what made you finally ask me to come be with you?"

It was a balmy Sunday evening, and we were sitting on the beach in the dimming twilight, relishing the calm after the exodus of day trippers. We'd swum earlier and dried off, and shed our swim suits, doing the under-towel shimmy. All I had on was a cotton wrap. He was bare-chested, with rough, draw-string trousers. A couple of locals had passed by, some with their dogs, and waved a greeting. Now there was no one left but us and the gulls swooping overhead. Felix was silent a while, puffing out his cheeks and thinking "You made a choice too," he said at last. "I could ask you the same question — what made you agree to come?" Fair enough, but I let him continue. "I think it was this: I thought I was about to kick the bucket, and I had only one regret — that I'd let fear keep me from you."

"Fear? Nonsense! You've never been afraid of anything in your life."

"I was afraid of you, Sally." He frowned, insistent.

"Remember that weekend out on Long Island? It was so clear to me then: You had your rules and I didn't trust myself to stick to them. I'd screw up and you'd write me off. You'd end up hating me. I couldn't bear to let that happen."

"What changed?" I scooped up a handful of sand and let it sift through my fingers, waiting for his answer.

"Death. Life. Knowing that little balloon in my brain could burst at any time. I had to take that risk."

"But it was still a risk?"

"Less than before. I might screw things up for myself, but I'm not scared of ruining your life anymore." I peered at him, baffled. "Well, I could ruin your old age, true. But not like when we were younger. You were so fragile, Sal, I was scared I'd scar you."

"I wasn't that fragile," I muttered. Maybe I wasn't, but something had stopped my coming after him, demanding what I wanted — at Greenport and even after that. It took facing the precipice for me too.

He leaned forward and linked his fingers through mine. I can still feel that dry, warm grasp. I miss it more than anything. He said, "All those years when we were apart, I thought about you often, and there were times when I dreamed about just swooping down and kidnapping you. But I knew it wouldn't work out."

"And now?"

"Well, you're old enough to make your own risk assessment. And you're tougher. You've been through a lot."

He gave a rueful grunt. "Plus, I trust myself more. The parts that used to have a will of their own — that got me into trouble — well, you might have noticed they don't have a will of their own anymore. It takes a lot to get the motor running these days, and all the parts have to work together — heart and mind, and vas deferens."

I shifted closer and linked my arm through his. The old me — or rather the young me — would have fished for a compliment, said something like, "It's understandable if I don't turn you on the way I used to..." But Sally 2.0 was wiser, thank God. I winked at him like a lascivious tart. "You could still make my parts work pretty well, old man, even if I need a bit of extra lubrication."

He laughed and kissed my sandy hand, and made a disgusted "sprrrat" sound. I grabbed his hair, longer than mine now, and pulled him to me, grit and all. He rubbed his nose against mine and our mouths came together. His fingertips glided over my nipple and rested there, his thumb stroking slowly across the thin fabric. The surrounding flesh might be softer than before, but that nub was still responsive. He eased me down onto the sand and leaned over me, kissing seriously now, his lips warm and salty. His hand slid under the edges of my wrap and up my inner thigh. I gasped, my back arching as it hadn't in years. He leaned over me, warm and sheltering, and

I tilted my pelvis up to welcome him.

"This is nuts," I said. "We're in public. Someone will see us."

"Who? It's dark and the only people who might come down here have the same action in mind."

"Then hurry," I said. Silly thing to say, but I tugged the string of his trousers loose, and he shoved them open, freeing himself. He began to press into me. I wiggled a little to assist, and he tried, but we couldn't quite achieve entry. I drew away just enough to reach down and start stroking and tightening. He groaned softly, moved my hand aside and pushed inside me. The roar and hush of the waves merged with the rush in my ears and the rhythm of his thrusting. And when we came, his cry in my ear was like the sound of the gulls.

"Remember the chicken and the egg?" I asked Felix as he rolled onto his back. It took a moment, and then he brayed with laughter until he had to sit up to catch his breath.

~ 20 ~

A Song

Just what does one gain from growing old? There's a blank diary in the drawer under the coffee maker with nothing written in it, one of those with days of the week but no dates, so you can use it for any month and any year. Not the kind Felix liked. Bought by mistake? Perfect for me.

Sitting barefoot at the kitchen table, I feel Mergatroid wind warm around my chilled ankles, giving a little love to her human, and a hint. I tell her, "I'll give you a treat, mama. In a moment." I start writing, making a list.

More self-knowledge? Yes. Less defensiveness? Yes. Aches and pains? Shit, yes. Hormonal upheaval? Pleasantly absent.

Resignation? Perhaps; so much has been lost, there is less left to fear. Who'm I kidding? Talk about a work-in-progress!

I draw a box around that summary, go into the bedroom, and squeeze the book into the box with Felix's journals.

But then I change my mind and take it out again. Joanie or Trevor should have the journals. Now I've got my own volume to start filling. I take it back to the kitchen. I want it on hand when I have my morning coffee.

Then I feed the cat. It's peaceful, just us two, while the kittens sleep. Will I be able to take her with me where I go?

I don't know what's going on with Joanie. She's smug about something. Usually, that girl can do no wrong in my eyes, even when she's cross with me, but I got irritated yesterday afternoon. She had a smirk on her face, and I caught her casting glances at me. When I said, "You look like a cat full of cream. What's going on?" she just said, "I don't know what you're talking about. I'm just happy being here with you." It's on her face again this morning first thing, in the deep curl at the corner of her mouth, just like her father's.

Maybe it's having Eric with her. They have disappeared for a couple of long walks along the main road, and yesterday they hiked in Silvermine Forest. They came back grubby and exhausted, and Eric showed me some spectacular pictures he took of the views, and also of the tiny, unexpected glories in the rocks and crevices. I like this guy. He'll be a tender father.

After breakfast today, he came to me with a request. Very tentatively, he said, "Sal, please feel free to say no if you prefer, but would it be all right if I took Felix's bike out for a spin? I have one like it back in San Francisco, and Joanie can tell you

225

I'm a competent rider. I'd love to take the day and do the whole coastal road."

I was squatting by Mergatroid, stroking her head and watching her brood competing for nipple access. Each time one clambered too far in the wrong direction, she stretched a little and nudged it back in the right direction. I was inclined to do the same thing, not to let this boy take any risks. But you can't do that with a grown-up.

"Look on the hook by the front door. I think Felix's keys are still there. But you have to use a helmet. There are two in the garage. One of them should fit you." He thanked me and trotted off with an air of purpose. Seeing him go, it dawned on me that with my joints feeling so much better, it might be fun to ride again. I could try the Harley, see how it handles.

Now Joanie has come back into the kitchen, still in her long sleep tee. She crouches down, cooing over the slowly waking kittens. I ask her if I did the right thing, letting her husband go out on the bike. She nods, and there's that secretive look again.

I ask, "Did your dad ever take you on the bike with him?"

The question has been triggered by the very last part of his last journal, that Port Elizabeth/Grahamstown postscript. I read it this morning as I waited for the first pot of coffee to brew.

Apparently, he visited his parents en route to Rhodes from his base at John Latimer's in Cape Town. It was the first time in all those years since leaving home, and he'd planned it with his mother.

He wrote:

*"The old sod hasn't changed. He answered the door
and said, "What are you doing here?" I said I came
to see Mom. She ran in from the kitchen and we
hugged. She looked scared Dad and I would hit each
other, but finally we shook hands. She's still dancing
to his tune. But when we were alone she made me
promise I'll come sometime when the others are
around. Maybe Easter. The worst part – when she
asked how I got there and I said by motorbike. On
my way out of town, left some wild flowers on J's
stone."*

J's stone?

Without answering my question about the bike, Joanie
stands up and pours herself a cup of coffee and holds up the
pot with raised eyebrows. I nod yes to a refill, maneuver myself
up from the floor, unfolding carefully, and join her at the
counter, looking out over the garden.

"No, I was never allowed on his bike," Joanie says at last.
"How about you?"

"Me neither, not once, not when we were at Rhodes, not
in these last few years, even after I became a rider myself. I've
never understood why. Do you?"

"He didn't say, but I've always assumed it was because of
Joanne," she said. "Isn't that why?"

I hold the warm mug up to my cheek as if that will help
still the tinnitus chiming in my ear. I blurt out, "Joanne? He
never told me anything about her, how she died, or why, or
when. What did she have to do with the motorbike?"

Joanie tilts her head, puzzled. "That's so weird – or maybe
not. I thought he told you everything. If he couldn't confide in

you, can you imagine how traumatic that whole thing must have been for him?"

"He told you." I still don't know what we're talking about, but here is the one woman in the world I'm perfectly happy to know Felix loved more than me, and maybe confided in more.

"Actually, no," she says. "I found out when we visited the family. My cousins told me. They showed me pictures of Joanne in our Granny Elsa's photo album, of her when she was a kid. I asked Dad about it, and he just said yes, that's what happened. I never said anything else about it; I just stopped asking him to take me on the bike."

"Joanie, for goodness sake, tell me what the connection is! What happened?"

She peers at me, still taken aback, and takes a deep breath. The ringing in my ears grows louder.

"Dad killed her, or that's what my cousins said our grandfather said. Not literally. Dad was riding and she was on the passenger seat. I don't know if they had helmets on. In those days the rules weren't so strict, were they? He hit a patch of water or oil or something, and he lost control of the bike. They said she was in the hospital for months before she died. Apparently, Dad wasn't hurt at all."

The explanation sifts slowly through my mind. Like a stain on a biologist's slide, it spreads across patches of memory, illuminates connections, and traces through threads of causation, of patterns and disruption. My chest aches.

Oh, my poor Felix, how did you bear that burden?

I want to reach back to Rhodes, to hug that wounded man-boy, to help ease the pain he didn't ever reveal, and yet — it's obvious now — showed in so many ways. How could I not have recognized it, not through all these years? His presence is suddenly so powerful here in this Kalk Bay kitchen, listening and shrugging, I almost turn to scold him.

Deep adjustments, and others too. Still seeking answers.

After I shower and dress for the day, I settle on the couch and again open Felix's last journal. Sure enough, squeezed in at the bottom of the last page in even worse than usual scrawl, there is one final passage apparently written after he came to Grahamstown. I make out the words: "*Registered today. So much damn paperwork. This might be a big mistake.*"

But just then the phone rings, and it's a friend who has a gorgeous garden. She says she spoke to Joanie but wants to double-check with me: Is it all right if she does the flowers for Felix's memorial party, something bright and colorful? Hadn't thought about flowers and I'm grateful. I want the room to look festive.

Is that what Joanie's smug smile is about? Surely not. I suspect that the kids are up to something. It better not be a birthday celebration. I turn sixty-nine today, and I'm hoping they don't know. I'm not ready to party, and I don't want any gifts. In any case, the memorial is coming up in less than a week. That will be party enough for me.

We've chosen our music and begun mapping out our little dance, practicing it bit by bit. The only conundrum is where to a find a third dancer. Eric has refused, though he is being helpful in other ways. I've even thought of asking Edith or Roxie.

Late in the afternoon, I head outside.

Funny, planting was never something I took an interest in before, not with Imma and Pops and obviously not through all the years of living in apartments. Liked flowers, loved being in the wild, but cultivating plants held no attraction. And here I am — though grateful that Jacob does the heavy work on his once-a-week visits — utterly contented, raking and digging, trimming and securing, preparing the soil for seeds I might not see grow.

Just as I'm stretching up, attempting to fasten a strip of old pantyhose to secure a bougainvillea stem to the trellis, I hear, "Let me help you with that." Two long, leather-clad arms reach above my head and tie the knot.

I step back baffled, instant calculation in process: *Too tall to be Eric. Rev. What's-his-name? No, too agile. Zac from next door?* I look again at the arms and gasp. That leather, scratched and scarred, with a couple of badges, so familiar. For a split second I think… and my head spins. But then I see a shock of curly hair above a pair of glistening topaz eyes: Trevor! And there behind him is Joanie, beaming her smug pussycat smile.

"When? Why didn't you tell me? How?" I hurl my arms around him, my cheek against his chest.

"Okay, okay, calm down. No heart attacks. We don't need to lose you as well." He hugs me back, and I can feel the laughter shaking him.

"I sent you that jacket all the way to California just so you could bring it back here?" It's a little shorter than on his dad but looks very good.

We three subside into the canvas deck chairs, and the siblings explain their scheme.

"We need another dancer, don't we?" Joanie says, pointing and entwining her feet. "So, I called Trev Tuesday last week after you'd gone to sleep. I knew he was considering coming, but he needed a prod. You know he can dance, don't you? Not ballet or anything, but for a guy his height, he's surprisingly light on his feet, like Dad was."

"Got his genes — or yours, Sal, by osmosis," he declares, and turns serious. "I wasn't going to come — not with Dad gone, but I felt so uneven. I really needed to be here, to be with you guys. My job gave me bereavement leave, and my *muma* wired me money for the ticket. She sends her love, by the way, and said to say she's thinking of us all."

Joanie's mother Deidre sent a card with a one-line message. I wouldn't expect more of her. But Nellie I like. In her way, she was good to Felix and good for him. She has called a number of times just to commiserate.

Trevor — just the age Felix was that first year at Rhodes — has his dad's ability to talk to anyone, but — unlike Felix — he's willing to chat about them too. He regales us with anecdotes about his Jamaican grandmother and the food packages she sends him. It reminds me of Imma and the treats she would send me, convinced I was starving without her. Trevor laughs when I tell him that and reminds me that I made pierogis for him and Joanie when they visited me in Brooklyn "a gazillion years ago."

He describes a couple he befriended on the plane and asks if it would be all right to invite them to come have lunch with us. "Hey, now I'm hungry," he exclaims. "Will you cook your Polish specials that day?"

It's getting chilly outside. I draw the kids into the house, and we start making dinner together, Joanie washing vegetables, Trevor peeling and slicing, me stirring things into the big cast iron pot. As we work, we brainstorm about our dance and how we would like the rest of the ceremony to go.

The hall at the church will be full. A surprising number of people have responded to the notice we posted on line. Angie is insisting on driving down from Grahamstown, and she is picking up our old pal Bev on the way. Isabelle is coming with accountant Stan. I called her to make sure, and let her tell me how brave I am and how much she admires me. Even old John Latimer says he plans to attend.

To my delight, Winston and Lindi, who're out from the States for a family wedding in Johannesburg, are coming down to Cape Town specially for our gathering. I can't wait to see them, and it pleases me greatly that they feel comfortable back here. As I kept telling Felix, some things have gotten better. Winston says he can't wait to see our dance.

There's sizzling and the aroma of onions and garlic and mushrooms and the sweet wheat smell of the chicken pot pie Joanie made earlier, baking in the oven. Eric joins us just in time to pour his wife some sparkling water and a glass of wine for me. He pops open beers for himself and Trevor.

Evidently the brothers-in-law were in cahoots. They rode back from the airport together on the Harley, "wearing the helmets," Eric assures me. "I took them both."

He adds, "By the way, done deal on the house. We're all in agreement. If you'll stay, we'll all keep coming. This is what Felix wanted. He made that really clear to all of us." The three of them look at me, beaming, and lift their drinks. I just hold mine up too, nodding and shaking my head, speechless, and sniff hard.

In that one statement, the march of time has been altered for me. From lurching forward into a dark unknown, it has swerved into a gentle arabesque, bound by memory and happy anticipation. The house, notwithstanding its drafts and leaks, this sheltering shell – with its kooky sailing motifs and all – is embracing all of us.

One of Mergatroid's kittens, the stripy ginger one, wobbles through from the kitchen, tiny feet splayed out, mewing. Joanie hands Eric her glass and slithers down onto the carpet to corral it before it gets lost under something. I sink onto the sofa with Trevor alongside me. He reaches out and envelopes my hand in his big paw, kisses it, and lets go. I sit there, watching them laughing and chatting – my family.

Joanie is making plans for tomorrow, for an excursion to the winelands. I'm itching to get to my new desk – the driftwood table in the attic – to start exploring Felix's material for the book, but they insist I come too. Of course, I agree. It's a weird feeling, being torn this way between desirable options.

My fingers, fiddling between the seat cushion and the padded arm, encounter the journal I was reading this morning. I open it at the last page again, remembering how close Felix and I came to never meeting, if he had decided to give up on Rhodes before he even began. He always hated paperwork.

"*But got talking to a gorgeous little redhead,*" he wrote. The handwriting is a sleepy scrawl, but I have become adept at deciphering his hieroglyphics. "*A dancer of course, shy but very direct. A weird, vibrating feeling when we looked at each other. Now I want to stay."*

Ahhhh. Exhale, and then inhale deeply, taking in that reality and this one, kittens and all. Eric slips a disk into the CD player. I wait to hear what he has selected. Joanie says, "Something for your birthday, Sal. We saw the little harmonica on the mantelpiece, thought maybe you'd like to hear that tune Dad used to play all the time."

It's the Elvis Presley song. I hum along, the sweetness spreading like heat, tightening my throat. The words sound different this time. Still about a guy stealing away while his lover lies sleeping, but I have finally absorbed the fact: My guy didn't leave willingly.

And with that thought, the well overflows, sending tears rinsing down my cheeks and into the soggy collar of my sweater. I fumble for a tissue. The kids, if they notice, aren't perturbed.

I love you, Felix. Always have. Always will.

It doesn't matter that he didn't ever say it, or that I didn't either. We have shared everything that counts except more time – and that's all right.

We share all this. Always will.

Preview of Sequel

LAF
Life after Felix

Elaine Durbach

~ *1* ~

When you have loved someone your entire adult life, how on earth are you meant to go on without them?

Just move on, Sal. You have so much to live for.
Easy for you to say, Felix; you did "move on."
Not by choice, and you know it.

Crazy lady here, talking to her departed lover – but not out loud. I'm not that crazy. Hearing him inside me. Feeling the love I doubted for so long. Still arguing with him.

Why are you so afraid today?
Who says I'm afraid?

But he's right, as usual. I am jittery and anxious. That agitation got me out of bed this morning earlier than in months, and out here into the garden.

It's hot already and the plants look dusty, neglected. How could I let this happen? Cape Town is in a drought, so we're not supposed to use hoses. Instead, I find the hand shovel under a pile of rusting implements and, contrite and clumsy, start chiseling into the hardened soil. Carve small hollows around the stems the way Jacob taught us, and – with a pitcher filled in the kitchen — dole out cautious portions of water. Hoping it will soften the soil, allow nourishment to reach the roots.

Yes, I know, I should have been doing this all along.

When Felix was here, we gardened together. It was a delight, even when we bickered over what to plant or how to prune. "Dabbling with nature's alchemy," he called it. In all the decades since we'd last lived together, way back in our youth, I hadn't cultivated anything larger than a window box of petunias. He hadn't either, till he asked me to come stay with him here in this ramshackle old cottage. He'd let the plants grow wild, the same way he'd let the ocean mist rust the window catches and the lichen spread over the roof tiles. But together we were making progress, indoors and out.

. . . till Felix died, in the middle of the night, eight months ago. Almost nine.

The shovel goes still, resting in a shadow.

Left me with no warning, no goodbye. Just a final flare in his marvelous brain — and gone.

We had only had five years together this time around. It wasn't enough. A hundred years wouldn't have been enough.

> *I was grateful every day of those five years.*
> Me too.

For all these months, hibernation has seemed the safest option. Reluctant even to come out here with the plants. I've hugged my loneliness like a shawl, doing my best not to care about anything, except the cats. Mergatroid and Skelm keep me company. Most days, unless my neighbors come by, I talk to no one except them — and Felix.

I'm not into supernatural stuff, haven't ever gone to seances or things like that, so what is this? Are his words just projection on my part, knowing him so well that I can predict what he'd say in any situation? But then what of the times when he catches me by surprise? Or when he nags me in a way he never used to?

> *Like about lightening up? You really need to.*
> *Sometimes, I think you love me more in absentia . . .*
> Nonsense.

Well, maybe. I did adore Felix in person, but his absence etches each detail of what is missing, every quirk and precious quality. Is it ever possible to appreciate someone with this intensity when they're alive, with you, face to face?

I pine for his physical presence. Hearing him helps, but I long to have his breath in the air I breathe, his weight in our bed, his arm tight around my waist, making me dance a silly jig. I still pour two cups of coffee each morning, so as not to see one alone on the table.

As the coffee brews, I write in my diary. Felix kept a journal, meticulously tracking the discoveries and ideas that filled his waking hours—as if he knew how abruptly it all could end. His entries were filled with passion, just like those he wrote way back in his youth, before we met, when he was traveling the world.

My entries are more mundane. I write so that my days don't merge into grayness. There's been so little to record – until the day before yesterday.

The first encounter, was that only forty-nine hours ago?

One hour till the second encounter. Trying to distract myself with this gardening, wanting to stall, to hide. I'm not ready for more of the disruption my visitor has wrought already.

The water seeps away as if it was never there. Should I cheat and use the hose? Can't, still too law-abiding. The marigolds and bougainvillea will probably survive, but the petals of the yesterday-today-and-tomorrow crumble as I touch them, releasing sweetness like a cheap perfume.

This is all my fault. Ridiculously, tears well up and trickle down the side of my nose. I wipe them away with muddy fingers. I should go inside and clean up. Maybe he'll call and cancel. I hope so.

As I stand up, Jacob calls a greeting from over the fence. This is his day to work at Edith and Roxie's next door. He used to come once a week to help us with the garden. I can't afford to pay him these days, but when he has time, he still stops by to check on me. He has a wonderful way of conveying sympathy without pity.

Jacob came to Felix's wake/memorial – whatever you want to call it – as did a motley collection of other guests of all races and ages. The event ought to have been far sooner. Felix's priest buddy, Bob Halpert, kept nagging me, though neither of us belonged to his flock, me being Jewish and my beloved a total freethinker. "You need closure," the reverend insisted. I disagreed, but I knew I owed it to all those as shocked as I was by Felix's sudden departure.

So, when his children came to visit from the States, my wonderful sort-of step kids Joanie and Trevor, and Joanie's husband Eric, I finally gave in. We did the deed together. It was a rollicking, drunken affair with lots of singing. We even choreographed a little dance, the kids and I, a brief piece to honor – and mock –their father, playing with the hats that were his trademark. It was the kind of party Felix Barnard would have loved.

That was the last time I've danced. And despite Bob Halpert's assurance, the party provided no closure. If anything, the gap loomed larger. A week later, Joanie, with her pregnant belly just starting to show, departed with her guys, heading home to America. I was left alone, hearing only my tinnitus and the wind rattling the windows – and occasional teasing taunts from my ghost lover.

I've tried to dance to lift my energy, as I have all my life. You don't have to be happy to find pleasure in rhythm, but you do have to let feelings flow through you, and that has seemed dangerous, as if something might tear.

Other than walks down to the sea or up the mountain, I've kept busy with tasks. Fixing this and that around the house. Sifting through Felix's stuff, giving away or throwing out whatever I can bear to part with. Trying to work on our long-delayed book, his and mine, about the benefits of dance. The fixing has gone quite well, the throwing out not so well, and the writing? Not well at all.

> *What else can you expect?*
> With the writing? Or from the unexpected visitor?

∽

As I wash and dress, details from Wednesday flicker through my mind, still intertwining disbelief and wariness.

This is what happened: Around mid-morning, I heard a

ding-dong at the front door. Opened expecting to see the mailman or a neighbor, and there stood – Felix?

For one glorious, breath-stealing moment, the impossible seemed possible. A great gust of relief filled me. Of course, it had just been a nightmare, a crazy illusion! Ground and sky swirled around me, and I had to clutch the door handle to keep from falling.

A man with a white Panama hat was smiling down at me. His cheeks creased the right way. He tilted his head the right way, peering inquiringly. Even the lilting timbre of his voice was right.

Then he whipped off his hat with an "Oops, sorry, ma'am!" That shook me awake. Felix would never have said that. And he'd have kept his hat on. The hair was thicker, more blond than gray. The eyes were different – not tiger topaz, more of a sea blue, or green. Hard to tell, and I was too flustered to decide.

I just croaked, "Yes? What can I do for you?"

"Are you Sally Paddington?"

"That depends. Who are you?"

The wind was blowing so hard, his answer whisked away from my ears, and I had to brace the door to prevent it from slamming shut. The buxom wooden mermaid above the lintel rattled on her hooks.

"May I come in?" he shouted. "It's kind of hard to talk like this."

"No."

I was still reeling, trying not to stare – not to look at him straight on, because I wanted so much to recapture that first blissful illusion. "I don't let strangers into my home. What do you want?"

"It's a bit awkward. A long story. What if I buy you a cup of tea at that café around the corner?"

It was a reasonable suggestion. With half my mind I recognized that. The other half was tumbling into the past, tripping over an echo; Felix said almost exactly the same thing to me all those eons ago, standing in line to register for the new college year back in Grahamstown, at Rhodes University. I could still feel the tingle that shimmied through me and the feeling of a passage opening to the future.

I told the man to give me a minute and closed the door, leaving him outside. Considered putting on a bra and changing out of my jeans and Felix's gray T-shirt, but instead just put on my green glass pendant, like a talisman. Tried to get a brush through my knotted white locks and gave up. Twisted my hair up instead, and with trembling hands fastened it with the first thing I found, a red clip that used to match my color.

Copper Girl, relax. It's okay.

Felix loved my hair when we met. Used to pull the pins out of my tight, neat knot so the waves would tumble down. He'd wrap the strands across his fingers and watch the light glisten off them. When at last we were together again, when my hair had faded to peach and then beyond, he didn't seem to notice the difference. I was still his Copper Girl.

So, who is he? I asked the air.
Find out.

Of course, Felix would say that.

I closed the front door and went to the café with the stranger.

On our way down the street, we passed Jacob, still trimming the hedge. He waved, and then did a double take, staring open-mouthed at my companion. I nodded, knowing what he was wondering, and waved back. I hoped he hadn't noticed the flush burning in my cheeks.

The man beside me had put his hat back on, though he had to hold it to withstand the gale. In the periphery of my vision, he looked utterly familiar. More real than real, almost glowing. Not quite as bowlegged as Felix, but with the same rolling cowboy gait that made my guy recognizable from blocks away. A wave of longing rippled through me, mingled with sharp curiosity.

"In case you haven't realized, I'm Humphrey Barnard," he'd said, as we set out down the street. Yes, this person was Felix's brother. I had guessed that already, but the confirmation reverberated through me. We'd never met before and I hadn't seen a clear picture of him in years, yet I knew every plane of his face.

Why had he come? If I remember correctly, in ancient Jewish lore it was incumbent on a man to marry his brother's widow. My education in these matters is sparse. It shouldn't be, given that my parents, both Holocaust survivors, subjected me to Hebrew school. But neither they nor I delved deep into the Bible. I learned more from Felix, steeped as he was in Evangelical Christian teaching that he had largely rejected. It was he who told me the bit about brothers, that it was to ensure the dead man's line continued if his wife hadn't yet borne him any children. But what if the widow and brother-in-law didn't like each other? And what if she was way past child-bearing age? Such a loopy notion, yet it yammered in my brain.

Humphrey certainly hadn't come with the aim of luring me into holy matrimony. Come to think of it, Felix didn't either; he and I never bothered to get married. Both too burnt by unsuccessful attempts during our years apart – two on his side, one on mind. So, I'm not legally his widow, and this Barnard surely had no intention of filling his sibling's shoes – or bed. I couldn't imagine what had brought him to me.

Humphrey? That came as a shock. Felix always called him Boet or Boetie, Afrikaans for brother. Joanie and Trevor referred to him as Uncle Boet. The youngest of the three boys, I remembered, was Matthew, but I had had no idea what this middle son's real name was. Ridiculous, yes, but Felix seldom spoke of them. In the early days, he just called them "the Neanderthals." He didn't talk about his two sisters either. It was a part of him that mystified me and still does, something oddly detached in a man who was warm with everyone else.

Now that name proved to be the first hurdle to our communication. When I heard the truth, I burst out laughing. In my defense, I was a bit hysterical, but who calls their child Humphrey? I asked that as we faced each other across a table in the café.

"The same people who named their first daughter Olivia, after their favorite movie star," he replied, "and their first born after a cartoon cat."

So that was where "Felix" came from. I'd always wanted to ask and – like with so much else – had been too circumspect to push for answers. "Perhaps, before they became who they became, they were impetuous kids with a sense of humor," this son told me. And here was another difference: Felix had never said anything that affectionate about his parents.

Our tea arrived, along with two oven-warm muffins. Humphrey inhaled deeply before taking a bite, relishing the aroma just as Felix used to. They smelled of vanilla with a hint of ginger, but my mouth was so dry I couldn't face eating anything. I gulped the too-hot Darjeeling instead.

"Who did they name you after?" I asked.

"Humphrey Bogart, another of their favorite actors." He licked crumbs from his lips. The corners of his mouth curled, just like those others I knew so well. I almost reached a fingertip to touch them. "Long story – for some other time."

There'd be another time?

He went quiet, staring at me as if wondering the same thing. "Your eyes are the same blue as my hydrangeas," he murmured. "Do you grow them too? Felix told me the two of you had become hotshot gardeners." I shook my head, admitting how negligent I've been. "I doubt that," he said. A flicker passed through me, as warm as a sip of whisky.

"We were learning as we went. But that 'long story' you mentioned . . .?"

"Oh, yeah, as I was saying: My folks planned to emigrate to the States, and they thought it would give us kids a leg up to have famous namesakes."

"Felix never mentioned that. He just told me about his adventures when he went in his twenties, before he came to Rhodes."

"Yeah, and then he went back a few years after you guys broke up," Humphrey added. He gave me an odd look. "Didn't you meet up by chance a while later, at some big event in California, in the 1980s?"

Everything around me seemed to fade, grow pale. What could he know of that encounter, or its consequences? Felix surely wouldn't have shared any of the details, and I had no intention of doing so either.

Instead, I asked, "Why didn't your folks ever go to America?"

"Not really sure. I think, by the time they could afford to, they'd lost heart. Been through too much loss. My mother just wanted to huddle in her nest and guard her remaining chicks." His openness astounded me.

A hush settled between us. Humphrey circled his mug with both hands and said, without looking up, "I suppose you want to know why I'm here."

I shrugged, suddenly wary. Why was he avoiding my gaze? Perhaps not so open after all. A chill spread across my scalp. The words blurted out: "Felix left everything to his children, to Joanie and Trevor."

Humphrey shoved himself away from the table, leaning the chair back on two legs as if to distance himself. "Shit, that's not why I came! I don't want his damn money, if he had any. On the contrary…"

Old Sally – well, young Sally – would promptly have apologized and tried to smooth things over, but this Sally didn't give a stuff. I've definitely become blunter as I age. "Don't get all huffy with me," I snapped. "What am I meant to think, you turn up like this without calling or texting? You didn't even attend his memorial party."

But I didn't want him to leave without telling me why he'd come. Didn't want him to leave, not so soon. My heart was hammering, maybe from the over-steeped tea. He brought the chair forward again, and I sucked in a deep breath, relieved.

"Fair enough," he said. "It's complicated. That's why I didn't call first. I had to be in Cape Town for work, and I thought I'd give it a try. Rented a car for the day and came. Helga, my wife, said I should phone before or write or something, that it was rude to just show up, or that I might drive all this way out to Kalk Bay and find you'd gone off to America. Isn't Joanie about to have her baby? Helga said you might want to be with her. I know she's not your daughter, but . . ."

This guy was a chatterbox. So many words. Felix could talk up a storm if he was discussing his theories about healing and motion, but about personal stuff he was always terse. Humphrey lifted his mug, realized it was empty, and signaled for a refill – and then waved his hand, a change of mind. He's nervous, I thought, and softened. And he's married and knows about Joanie's pregnancy.

It's true, I've been thinking of going to the U.S., if I can scrape together the money and the courage to leave my cocoon. I'm not really comfortable around babies, haven't been for a long time, but I love Joanie and she has been hinting that I should come.

"You're in touch with the kids?" I asked.

"Now and then, since Felix brought them to visit Mom after my father died. He wouldn't come while the old man was around." I remember that saga, how their father had reacted to Felix having a son who was half-Jamaican.

Humphrey grimaced, then continued: "Joanie tells me she's closer to you than to her actual mother. That Deidre sounds like a bitch. Helga says I shouldn't judge, that I don't know what Felix did to piss her off, but that doesn't excuse her being a lousy parent. Trevor's mom, now she's a different story."

I remember feeling like a pendulum. One moment he annoyed me, the next I approved of his thinking. I like Nellie too.

"So why *are* you here?" I demanded.

He dipped his head and sighed. "I wasted too much time. And there's stuff I need to straighten out about Felix and my mom and our family before it's too late."

"Too late? Are you dying?"

He looked up and then guffawed. "Aren't we all? Thank the Lord, no, I'm fine. You really don't mince your words, do you? You're not what I expected. Joanie always said you were such a lady."

"So, what do you mean, 'too late'?" I'd been through losing one Barnard brother; if this one planned on exiting soon, I didn't want anything to do with him. My breath grew rough. This wasn't a joking matter for me.

"I have to be back in the city center for a meeting this afternoon," Humphrey said. "Actually, it's you I was worrying about."

"You've had a strange way of showing it." The waiter paused beside me with a tray of dirty dishes, and I clunked my mug onto it. Another pendulum swing. I wanted to leave, to get away. It's true that in the first weeks after Felix's death — even the first months — I'd contemplated suicide. It seemed to offer a sweet relief, a way to follow him. Some days it still feels like a good idea, but I'd never tell anyone. Humphrey couldn't possibly know, though the way he was looking at me now with those eyes the color of the sea, it was as if he did.

"I don't mean you're going to die," he said quietly. He laid his fingers on my wrist. I shivered. "Joanie said something about you maybe wanting to close this chapter, to move on. I thought you might move back to New York, that I'd lose the chance to meet with you."

I jerked my hand away. "She thought that? I never wanted to leave." It came out sharper than I intended. "We sorted that out before the memorial, before they went home to America."

"Like I said, I've only had sporadic contact . . ."

"I was surprised you didn't come. Joanie said she'd invited you all. Your brother and sister came. I don't understand why you didn't." I was on the attack, angry with him, I think, for the let-down after that initial moment of crazy hope.

"Hey, lighten up," he said. I wanted to reach across and slap him. Bad enough to have a ghost say that. "There's a lot I expect you don't understand." We glared at each other. He broke away and I saw him glance down at the pendant rising and falling with my panting breaths.

A voice came from above: "Sally Barnard — I mean Paddington! What a lovely surprise. So nice to see you out and about. And — oh, my goodness, you must be — Peter? Or was it Paul? One of the disciples. Felix's brother?"

"Yes, but not the disciple one, Matthew. Humphrey, actually." He got to his feet and held out his hand. "And you are?"

It was the minister, Bob Halpert, who'd recently become my buddy too. He was clad in black, as usual, but he'd swept up to us with such blithe benevolence, I could almost see his wings. I frequently almost spot a halo in the gleam around his bald head. Eyes wide, he pulled up a chair, and turned our duel into a sunny circle of pleasantries. Humphrey sat up straighter, his demeanor respectful. Bob asked about Port Elizabeth, where Humphrey lives, and about his work in marine biology, and about poachers and conservation, and on and on.

I wondered if the big brother had opened up with Bob as readily as the younger one was doing. I know Felix shared secrets he wouldn't discuss with me. I should have pushed harder for answers when he was around, sought to understand the wounded parts of him. Hard as I've tried to make my peace with those blank patches, they still bother me. Perhaps it's why his ghost hovers, because I keep asking.

And now here was this very-much-alive family member who simultaneously made things better and worse.

Finally, Humphrey looked at his watch. "Excuse me, Sally, Reverend Halpert. I must get going. I've got that meeting in the city. Sorry. This is nuts."

"Can you come back tomorrow? You never finished telling me why you came. And I have some things of Felix's that you might like to have." The moment the words came out my mouth I wanted to grab them back.

"Not tomorrow. We have an all-day conference in Stellenbosch." I turned away, looking for a waiter to pay. He said, "How about the next day? I'm meant to fly back first thing on Friday morning, but I can take a later flight. Please?"

I was about to tell him I was busy, that it wouldn't suit me. My guard had gone up. But I wasn't busy that day, or the next, unless you count my feeble attempts to work on the book. And, more urgent, I also have a conference I should be preparing for, unless I can squirm out of it.

But Humphrey was looking at me like an eager boy, almost pleading. "Yeah, you can come on Friday," I said. "Same time."

Forty-five hours to wait.

To be continued…

About the Author

Elaine Durbach published her first article at age five in the *Sunday Times* of Rhodesia (now Zimbabwe), where she was born. She grew up in Zambia and Lesotho and studied journalism at Rhodes University in Grahamstown, South Africa.

A World Press Institute Fellowship first brought her to the United States in her mid-twenties. Marriage brought her back, and she lives now in Maplewood, New Jersey, with her husband Marshall and son Gabe.

Elaine began writing fiction in 2013. She has completed two novels in addition to *Roundabout* and now its sequel *LAF ~ Life after Felix*. Until then, she had focused on nonfiction, writing news and feature articles for newspapers and magazines in South Africa and the U.S., most recently for *New Jersey Jewish News*. She has won three New Jersey Press Association awards. She has also written and published two non-fiction books – *With Mixed Feelings,* with photographer John Rubython and *South Africa, the Wild Realms,* with photographer Gerald Cubitt (both with Don Nelson Publishers).

❧ ❧ ❧